SCORPION: SECOND GENERATION

The colony of deadly scorpions at Long Point Nuclear Plant was eradicated. Or so people thought . . . Over a year later, entomologist Miles Ranleigh receives a worrying telephone call. A man has been fatally poisoned by toxic venom, identical to the Long Point scorpions' — but far more powerful. Miles and his companion Jill Ansty must race to destroy the fresh infestation. But this is a new strain of scorpion. Mutated and irradiated, they're larger, more savage — and infected with a deadly virus fatal to humans. And they're breeding . . .

Books by Michael R. Linaker
in the Linford Mystery Library:

SCORPION
THE TOUCH OF HELL

MICHAEL R. LINAKER

SCORPION: SECOND GENERATION

Complete and Unabridged

LINFORD
Leicester

First published in Great Britain

First Linford Edition
published 2007

British Library CIP Data

Linaker, Michael R.
Scorpion: second generation.—Large print ed.—Linford mystery library
1. Nuclear power plants—Fiction 2. Scorpions—Fiction 3. Animal mutation—Fiction
4. Suspense fiction 5. Large type books
I. Title
823.9′14 [F]

ISBN 978–1–84617–983–9

Published by
F. A. Thorpe (Publishing)
Anstey, Leicestershire

Set by Words & Graphics Ltd.
Anstey, Leicestershire
Printed and bound in Great Britain by
T. J. International Ltd., Padstow, Cornwall

This book is printed on acid-free paper

For Professor E. M. S. Symonds — with grateful thanks. Also for Matthew Edward and Robin Michael — like all good things well worth waiting for.

Prologue

. . . it was almost a three-hundred foot drop, straight down. Lemmy fell screaming all the way, his body turning over and over. The turning and the screaming ceased in the same instant. His body struck hard rock at the base of the cliff. The impact shattered every bone in his body, compressing flesh and organs. The skull burst apart like a smashed egg, brains spattering across rock, wiping out everything that had been Lemmy Tyson in one split second.

The scorpions clinging to Lemmy's body survived for the most part. Three of them were no more than pulpy smears, but five, entangled in Lemmy's clothing, crawled out of the sodden remains. They huddled together on the slimy surface of the rock until a wave crashed down and swept them out to sea . . .

. . . helpless in the grip of the rising sea the scorpions were lifted, tossed effortlessly through the white-crested waves.

Acting from the basest instinct for survival three of the scorpions — in the brief moments before the swelling waves separated them — drew together in a parody of an embrace, pincered arms entwining, bodies curving one around the other. The threat to their existence generated a need to rely on each other.

Like so much flotsam they were carried further and further away from the rocky shoreline, all sense of direction lost in the turbulent darkness. Place and time had no meaning. The sea, in its implacable mood of awesome superiority over all else, held anything and everything in its grip . . .

The motor-yacht *Southern Drift* challenged that formless might as it doggedly maintained its westerly course. Running speed had been considerably reduced since the change in the weather. The strong winds and driving rain had combined with heavy seas to create a difficult passage for the vessel. Sodden canvas had been exchanged for the steady pulse of the yacht's powerful diesel-motor, which now justified its existence by pushing the sleek vessel through the high-rising, hissing waves that constantly broke over the side-rails, washing the deck with glistening streams.

Again and again the boiling surge of water breached the sides of the yacht, bubbling and foaming as it crashed down on tightly-secured hatches and stowage lockers. A surging mass of water, rising well above the tilted deck, dropped heavily. The deck became awash, water beginning to run away almost immediately, leaving the smooth deck glistening wetly. As the yawing vessel regained its equilibrium, pale moonlight broke through the dense cloud to lay cold illumination across the deck, revealing three dark shapes scuttling rapidly across the open area.

Accepting that there was something solid beneath them once more, the surviving scorpions immediately sought out the darkest and warmest place available. An inner sense warned them of danger for as long as they remained in their present, hostile environment.

With the unerring instinct of the true survivor the scorpions located a dark, secure place to conceal themselves: a locker containing spare cable and rope, situated in the depths of the yacht. Below was the engine-compartment — a source of heat that rose to cocoon the interior of their hiding-place.

It warmed the three scorpions, soothing them to lethargy and enabling them to rest. They had already established the lack of any immediate threat and with that knowledge came an opportunity to recoup spent energy. To prepare themselves for what lay ahead . . .

Almost fourteen months have passed since the destruction of the Long Point scorpions. Fourteen months for the panic to have evaporated. For the concern to have faded. Time for the horror to have lessened its hold on frightened minds. Fourteen months . . . time enough to forget.

GENESIS

1

In the distance the church clock struck seven as Gillian Bampton closed the garden gate behind her. She paused for a moment to take in a breath of early evening air, contentment cloaking her. At her feet a small, bright-eyed Yorkshire terrier gazed up at her in anticipation, and Gillian found herself smiling.

'Off you go then, Timmy,' she said, and watched the tiny bundle of fur streak away across the narrow lane and down the grassy meadow on the far side.

Gillian followed the dog's trail. The warm air was scented with the tang of the sea which lay less than a half mile to the west. She walked slowly, savouring the solitude. Her days were spent behind the counter of one of Port Pendall's banks. Gillian enjoyed her work, but during the long summer weeks, when the holiday-makers flooded the area, the normally peaceful atmosphere was destroyed. Returning home each evening to the small cottage where she lived with her parents, Gillian would enjoy a leisurely meal and then take her dog for a walk.

Ahead of her she could see Timmy leaping about in the grass. She envied his moment of freedom, the abandoned wildness, and often tried to imagine how it must feel to be able to run so far, so fast.

She usually spent at least an hour on her walk if she wasn't going out anywhere. Her route took her along a footpath originally belonging to one of the old tin mines that had operated in the area in the late 1800s. Beyond the footpath the meadow gave way to wild moorland where gorse and bramble lay thick on the ground. Now it softened beneath the lowering sun, long shadows sliding across the undulating landscape.

She stopped suddenly, a frown darkening her pretty face as she caught sight of the terrier leaving the path to plunge into the dense thicket of the moor.

'Timmy! Hey, Timmy, you come back here!'

Quickening her pace Gillian reached the spot where the dog had disappeared. There was a break in the thicket and she eased her way through the tangled undergrowth, glad that she was wearing jeans.

'Timmy, where are you?'

Somewhere ahead she heard rustling in the thicket. Gillian smiled indulgently as she started for the spot.

'All right, Timmy, my lad! Come on out now! Game's over!'

The thicket rustled again. Gillian could see the interwoven brambles moving. She stood still. Surely, that couldn't be Timmy causing such a disturbance. He was too small. Far too small. He could work his way through the undergrowth without moving a single leaf.

Gillian experienced a moment of disquiet and decided to return to the path.

The undergrowth rattled violently.

Gillian stared intently at the spot. Now she was certain she could see something in there.

A bulky, dark shape pushing its way to

the edge of the thicket. Coming out into the open. Directly at her . . .

The closely woven bramble burst apart and the cause of the disturbance confronted her.

Gillian opened her mouth to scream, but the cold terror of the moment paralysed her vocal chords, rendering her incapable of expressing horror at the appearance of the nightmare creature before her. She began to back away, unable to break the hypnotic spell cast by the malevolent eyes that watched her every move.

The eyes were set in a long, dark body supported on eight bristled legs. At the forefront lay a flat head, the underside showing the moist gash of a mouth, from which glistening secretions dribbled over rows of sharp teeth. On either side of the head jointed appendages arched forward, each tipped with cruel, snapping pincers. At the rear, the tapering tail section curved up and over the creature's back, and protruding from the swollen, softly bulbous sac rounding out the tip, a slim needle — a sting.

Though Gillian would never know it, the creature menacing her was *Androctonus Australis*, one of the deadliest of the scorpion family.

But no scorpion in the living memory of man had ever looked like this. Its body was easily four feet long — with a two-foot tail swaying above its head and pincered arms as long as a man's. This scorpion was the progeny of the mutated survivors from Long Point. Scorpions that had eventually emerged from the cocoon of the yacht on which they had travelled, found themselves a hidden place in which to lay their eggs, and had set in motion the breeding cycle destined to produce a new strain of mutated scorpion. A new breed.

The second generation.

Gillian closed her eyes, shaking her head desperately. Hoping that when she opened them again the thing would have vanished. It hadn't; it had moved closer.

Oddly, there was hesitancy in its approach. Almost as if it was unsure of *her*. Maybe even afraid. Gillian saw a possibility for escape and knew she had to make the attempt or die.

The scorpion arched its body, raising itself on the eight, jointed legs, and as it moved the curving tail quivered, a gleam of moisture showing on the tip of the sting.

Tensing her muscles Gillian prepared to run for her life.

She only got as far as raising her right foot off the ground . . .

Something closed around her ankle. Tight. With enough force to penetrate the flesh to the bone. Agonising pain engulfed her foot and lower leg. Gillian bit back a cry of pain as the pressure increased and she felt the warm rush of blood flood into her shoe. Already off balance she tried to shake off the hold on her leg. Instead she was violently dragged to the ground, the breath driven from her lungs on impact. Stunned, she lay in an agony of immobility.

Ignoring the pain that burned its way higher up her leg, she twisted her protesting body so that she could look back across her shoulder. She found herself staring into expressionless eyes.

A ragged scream burst from her throat. The scorpion drew back fractionally — then lunged forward, releasing its grip on her ankle so that it could use both pincered arms. Gillian threw up her hands in an attempt to ward off the attack. It was a futile gesture.

The scorpion reared up, casting a dark shadow across her cowering body. And then it bore down using pincers and teeth to terrible effect. Soft flesh was torn apart, bright blood spurting, dappling the scorpion's shell-like body. Bone splintered under the sheer ferocity of the attack. The sudden presence of rich, warm blood incensed the scorpion and it rendered the writhing, moaning girl senseless. Only when she stopped moving did the creature cease the attack. It hovered over the mutilated corpse, then gripped the body with powerful pincers and began to drag it across the clearing and into the dense, tangled undergrowth . . .

Some time later a small dog emerged. It wandered back and forth across the clearing, occasionally stopping to sniff at the ground. Then it began to cast about excitedly, ears pricked up, shrill yelps filling the air. And just as swiftly the excitement evaporated and the dog began to whimper, pressing close to the ground, showing the whites of its eyes.

With a final howl of terror it turned about and raced away, back onto the old path, cutting off across country until it had lost itself in the hazy distance.

2

It had been the hottest summer on record. Endless weeks of blue skies and soaring temperatures.

In the south-west, the Cornish Peninsula was experiencing its best ever season. Holiday-makers, despite economic cutbacks and a multitude of other ills wished on them by the prophets of doom, had descended upon the area *en masse*. June and July had brought them by the thousand, and with August just commencing, more were still arriving.

Police Constable Trevor Parkinson eased the Panda car up to the kerb, cut the engine, and sat watching the surging crowds of tourists filling Port Pendall's main street. *Where do they all come from?* It seemed as though the entire population of the country was trying to cram itself into the small town. On the other hand, he had to admit that Port Pendall had taken on a new lease of life since the tourist explosion. Once a small fishing port, the town had been slowly dying. Then the leisure industry had wormed its way into Cornwall, opening up fresh channels that brought first a slow trickle, then a rushing flood of people willing to spend a lot of money for the privilege of enjoying the Cornish climate and tranquil pace of life. Early opposition had gradually faded, and though there were still some who regretted the yearly invasion, it had to be accepted that the holiday trade *did* bring a lot of welcome-business to the area.

Not that it was any consolation to the hard pressed police. During the season Port Pendall's seven and a half thousand population was increased to staggering proportions. It meant extra work, trying to keep traffic flowing through narrow, part-cobbled streets that had never been laid for use by motor vehicles. Added to that was the ever-increasing problem of providing parking spaces for the thousands of cars moving in and out of the town. Then there were the crowds themselves. People in a relaxed mood who only wanted to stroll along the quayside and gaze out across the blue, sun-glinting waters of Pendall Bay. They filled the winding streets, overflowing the pavements, and blocked the roads themselves. Occasionally there was the odd spot of bother stirred up by members of the rival motorcycle gangs who seemed to spend the summer chasing up and down the coast and stopping off in the various holiday spots.

Parkinson stirred uncomfortably in his seat as a runnel of sweat trickled down his back under his clinging uniform shirt. He hated being on duty during this hot weather. He always felt awkward, aware that the heat caused him to sweat a lot, leaving him damp and sticky. It was difficult to remain calm and detached when the legs of his trousers were stuck to him like flypapers.

He reached for the microphone of his car radio and called up his control. He told them his location and that he was leaving the vehicle for a while. They could contact him via his personal communicator. Climbing out of the car, Parkinson locked it, put on his uniform cap, and crossed the busy pavement.

The sign above the shop said: Henry Trevo Family Butcher. The Trevo family had sold meat to the residents of Port Pendall for over 150 years from the same shop. Little had changed, apart from the up-to-date equipment inside. Refrigerators, decimal cash registers and bright strip lights. The service was the same as it had always been, putting the customer before everything else — which was a novelty, Parkinson thought as he entered the shop.

'Can I help you?' an attractive, brown-haired girl asked from the other side of the counter. Like all the Trevo staff she wore the traditional blue and white striped apron over spotless whites, with a flat-brimmed straw hat perched on her head.

'I'd like a word with Mr Trevo,' Parkinson said, giving her a quick smile.

The girl nodded and slipped through a door at the far end of the shop. She returned quickly, followed by a big, smiling man, dressed in clothing identical to her own.

'The station asked me call in, sir,' Parkinson said.

Matt Trevo lifted the counter flap and ushered Parkinson through. 'I appreciate your prompt action,' he said. 'Mind, I don't know what you'll make of what I've got to show you.'

He led the way through the meat-cutting room at the rear of the shop and along a wide, tiled passage. At the end of the passage was a heavy wooden door. Parkinson recognised it as the door of the shop's cold-storage room. As they neared the door Matt Trevo stepped aside to let Parkinson by.

It was quiet for a while.

Then Trevo said: 'See what I mean?'

'When was this discovered?'

'This morning when the place was opened up. And to answer your next question — yes, it was fine last night. I was here myself until seven-thirty. Did the locking up, in fact. It hadn't happened then.'

Parkinson took off his cap and ran a hand through his damp hair. He crouched down and took a closer look.

‘How thick is this door? Couple of feet?’

‘Easily. And it’s locked each night.’

‘I’ll be honest, Mr Trevo, and say I couldn’t guess what did that. But from looking at it I’d say it’s been ripped open. Those bolts holding the locking bar in place have been *torn* out of the wood. But there aren’t any signs of any kind of leverage against the door itself.’

‘That’s the way I saw it. But that’s just not possible, is it? It would take more than a man’s strength to get hold of that bar and *rip* it free.’

‘Anything inside?’

Trevo smiled, almost as if he was enjoying the mystery. ‘Best part to come.’

He swung open the door and led Parkinson inside. Pale wreaths of white mist hung in the chilled air. Parkinson ran his eyes along the rows of hanging carcasses, then down to the floor and what lay there.

A half-dozen sides of beef had been dragged from the steel hooks on which they had been suspended. The meat had been torn and shredded from the bones.

Chunks of it lay strewn across the floor. Parkinson took a closer look. As with the door of the cold-store, the meat had been torn free. There was no indication of any neat knife cuts. The raw, frozen meat had been pulled off in chunks.

Parkinson stood up and drew his notebook from his hip pocket. He took out his pen, wondering whether the manufacturer's claim of his pen writing under water also applied to using it in sub-zero temperatures.

'For the moment, sir,' he said to Trevo, 'I'll take a few notes and we'll look into this.'

* * *

Just over one hour later Parkinson was driving along a rutted lane belonging to the Needham farm. Jim Needham had taken over after the death of his father a few years back. He was a young man, only a year older than Trevor, and the two had known each other for years. For a time they had been rivals, both of them pursuing the same girl. Needham had won and had married two years ago. The trouble was that Trevor had never quite got over his feelings for her. He still nurtured a deep longing, a longing which manifested itself in disturbing night-time fantasies.

Pulling up outside the rambling old farmhouse Parkinson climbed out of the car. He stretched lazily, arching his back. One of the drawbacks of having a country beat like his was the long periods spent behind the wheel of a car. It was good when he had the chance to stand upright and exercise his aching muscles.

The farm appeared deserted. Parkinson crossed the yard, making for the house. Before he reached it the front door opened and a familiar voiced called out to him.

'Hi there, Mr Plod!'

Trevor Parkinson felt a sudden jolt of excitement course through his body. He let his gaze linger on the lithe figure of the girl who stepped out of the house.

Linda Needham was a tall, attractive girl in her early twenties. She had jet-black hair that shone where the sun caught it. Her eyes were a startling blue and regarded the world with a frankness that could be off-putting. Today she was wearing a pair of tiny shorts and a faded red T-shirt easily two sizes too small; somehow she had managed to get the shirt on and the effect was to say the least unnerving. Parkinson found it difficult to shift his gaze from the shape of her full breasts that moved constantly beneath the taut cotton.

'Were you looking for me, Trevor?' Linda asked.

'Well . . . no . . . it's Jim I'm after.'

'I should be offended at that last remark,' Linda smiled. 'But seeing as it's you, Mr Plod, I'll forget it. Anyway, Jim isn't here. He had to go over to Penzance and I'm not expecting him back until tonight.' She made no attempt to conceal the annoyance she was feeling. 'Stuck here all day by myself,' she added, grumbling softly. Then: 'Was it important?'

Parkinson shrugged. 'I don't know. Jim asked me to call by. Said something about vandals tearing down some fencing on his top-field. And there was something about him missing some livestock.'

'Oh that!' Linda reached out and took his arm, guiding him to the house. 'Give me a few minutes to put some clothes on and I'll show you the broken fence.'

She had to press close to him as they went in through the door and Parkinson became acutely aware of the pressure of her left breast against his arm. Even through the sleeve of his shirt he could feel the soft warmth of her flesh. Glancing down, Parkinson found that he could clearly see the half-erect nipple through the shirt. It was only when Linda spoke that he realised she was aware of his close scrutiny.

'Is it bothering you?' she asked.

He raised his eyes to her lovely face, knowing that his cheeks were flushed and warm.

'I . . . er . . . '

Linda laughed heartily. 'You always did blush easily, Trevor, my lad.'

'You can't expect people not to stare when you're . . . '

This time her laughter filled the

hallway. 'When I'm exposing myself you mean!'

'Well it's . . . ' he began.

'You never complained when we were dating. If I remember correctly you were always trying to get my clothes off!'

Parkinson smiled at some long-forgotten, revived memory of lazy summer evenings spent walking along deserted clifftops, or the frequent lovemaking in the sandhills that were still warm from the long day's sun. The memories came flooding back in an erotic jumble and Trevor Parkinson felt himself giving in to distinctly physical emotions.

'Linda, I . . . ' he began, his voice hoarse.

'Still want me, don't you, Trevor?'

Linda had moved further along the hallway.

'Close the door, Trevor,' she told him, a slow, secretive smile playing around the corners of her shapely mouth.

Parkinson turned and closed the door. When he looked back he saw that she had removed her T-shirt. Her naked, full breasts moved soft and heavy, dark nipples standing erect and large.

'He won't be back until tonight,' she reminded him, then turned and began to climb the stairs. Before she was halfway up she had unzipped her shorts and pushed them down until they slid to her ankles. At the top of the stairs she faced him, standing with her slim hands resting lightly on her thighs.

'Coming, Trevor?'

Her voice floated down, gently taunting him. With one foot on the first stair he raised his eyes, letting his gaze slide up her long, superb legs, thighs parted slightly, the dark curl of soft pubic hair shadowing the moist swell of her vagina.

'Trevor . . .'

He moaned softly to himself, and thought, I'm going to feel bloody lousy about this later — but then he couldn't do anything about that now. He began to climb the stairs to where Linda was waiting for him . . .

It was two hours later when Linda drove him up to the top-field in the farm's Land Rover. Neither of them had spoken since leaving the house. Parkinson, after the frenzied passion of the last hour or so, found himself confused and extremely unsure as to how he was going to handle the situation that had unexpectedly arisen. Despite his misgivings he had found his sexual encounter satisfying to a high degree. His experience of Linda before her marriage had shown him that she was a capable and inventive partner. Yet that knowledge had not prepared him for the intensity of her performance. Time had aroused passions that must have lain dormant during their affair. He'd wondered briefly whether marriage to Jim Needham had been the catalyst; had Jim taught her the tricks she was using on him? Thinking about Jim, his friend, had instilled a shadow of guilt, and he'd paused in his lovemaking, his mind suddenly whirling with conflicting emotions. He had failed to notice Linda's frustrated stare until she had poked him in the ribs.

'Hey, don't stop now,' she'd whispered, her voice heavy with emotion. Even as she spoke she was moving her hips, arching her body as she sought to maintain the contact of his rigid penis against the sensitive inner membrane of her swollen vagina. She was in an extreme state of sexual arousal. Close to a climax and determined not to lose the feeling. Her persistence had drawn him back, taking him along with her, leaving him drained and still confused.

'Over there,' Linda said, her voice breaking his train of thought.

Parkinson followed her pointing finger. As the Land Rover approached the fence edging the field he could see where the damage lay. It was the custom for Cornish farmers to border their fields and property with dry stone walls, so this one section of Needham's farm was an exception to a rule. The fencing along this top-field had been in place for over sixty years; thick oak posts and cross-pieces that had withstood both time and the elements.

As the Land Rover stopped Trevor Parkinson climbed out and went to inspect the broken section. One upright had been snapped off a foot above ground and a row of cross-pieces had been ripped free and scattered about in a haphazard fashion, broken splinters of wood littering the immediate area. Parkinson examined the upright. He was aware of the strength of a solid oak post and knew it would have required a lot of force to break it.

If his attention had been fully concentrated he might have realised the parallel between this incident and the one at the Trevo butcher shop. He might also have noticed unusual scuff marks in the dry, dusty earth on the far side of the fence. However, Trevor Parkinson had other things on his mind. Returning to the Land Rover he climbed in, closing the door.

'You said something about missing livestock?'

Linda nodded. 'Couple of ewes.'

'I've seen enough,' Parkinson said. 'Run me back down to the farm.'

As she drove back towards the distant farm Linda glanced across at him. 'When?' she asked.

Parkinson looked up from his notebook. 'When what?'

'I want to see you again.'

'Linda, we could be making a lot of trouble for ourselves.'

'Don't tell me trouble bothers *you*!'

'It hasn't got anything to do with that and you know it.'

'Well, let's not get too intense about it, then. Look, Trevor, it wouldn't have happened at all if things were right between Jim and me. So don't get all moral or anything like that. It was bound to happen sooner or later. The best thing about it is the fact that it happened with you.' She reached out and laid her hand across his, fingers gripping tightly. 'I made a mistake marrying Jim. It just hasn't worked. I've known that for months. Today proved how right I've been.'

'Let's hope so,' Parkinson said.

On his return to Port Pendall, Trevor Parkinson was diverted from reporting to his station. A call over the radio sent him to the scene of a road accident. Two cars and a heavy lorry had been involved in a collision at the junction of the main road and two minor roads on the outskirts of town. All three roads were blocked with traffic and Parkinson was forced to drive his car along the wrong side of the road and then abandon it a hundred yards short of the junction. He switched on the hazard-flashers and roof-light before making the rest of the journey on foot. He found his own station sergeant already there, trying to help a passenger trapped in the crumpled wreckage of one of the cars. Within a couple of minutes Parkinson found himself directing the lines of traffic in an attempt to clear the blockage.

It was a long and tiresome task, made even more difficult by the stifling heat, impatient drivers and the urgency of making a way for the ambulances that were on their way to the scene. It took over three hours to get the situation under full control. By this time other units had arrived. Parkinson was relieved and able to make his way home. He was already off duty — had been for two hours. By the time he reached his small flat, overlooking the harbour, weariness dictated his actions. He took a quick shower and fell into bed.

The following morning found him filling out the endless reports that were a legacy of the previous day's accident.

The reports and the follow-up occupied his attention to such a degree that he didn't have time to think about Linda Needham, or what had taken place. He also forgot about the minor grievances of Jim Needham and his broken fence *and* Matt Trevo's damaged cold-store door.

3

'Now can you hear it?'

The voice penetrated Don Ransome's sleep drugged senses. He rolled over onto his side, pressing close to the warm, velvet flesh of the girl lying beside him. Automatically he slid an arm across her naked body, the fingers of his hand coming to rest against the full swell of a breast.

'Cut it out, Don!'

A faint stirring of annoyance intruded on Don's thoughts and he felt his sleepiness drifting away. He sighed, knowing that he wouldn't be allowed to settle again until he had satisfied her curiosity.

'All right!' he mumbled, kicking the sheets aside. He sat up, yawning, trying to clear his head. Glancing at his watch he saw that it was two-thirty. Bloody ridiculous!

The bed creaked softly as the girl sat

up, brushing strands of tawny-blonde hair away from her tanned face.

'Thanks,' she said as she swung her long, bare legs to the floor. Crossing the small bedroom she eased back a corner of one curtain, peering out into the moonlit garden that surrounded the old cottage.

Don joined her, finding it difficult to concentrate on anything other than her naked and very desirable young body. The pale moonlight coming in through the window provided enough illumination to reveal the slim curve of one hip and tautly-rounded buttock.

'I can't see a damn thing out there,' he said. 'Or hear anything.'

Terri Sheldon turned to stare at him, her face set in a determined expression. 'I wasn't hearing things, Don. You know I'm not the sort to get jittery over nothing.'

Don nodded. She was right there. Terri Sheldon was the most well-adjusted female he'd ever come across. She had a sensible, logical outlook on life, and had little time for hang-ups or phobias. Added to that, she was also clever, witty *and* beautiful — in and out of bed.

‘I’ll take a look,’ he said, wandering out of the bedroom and down the short flight of stairs to the living-room. He heard the soft sound of bare feet following close behind him.

‘I’m not staying up there on my own until we’ve sorted this out,’ Terri said forcibly.

‘Fine,’ Don told her as he flicked on the light.

They crossed to the front door. As Don unlocked it he heard Terri stifle a giggle.

‘What’s wrong now?’

‘Nothing, lover,’ she said, unable to hold back a smile.

‘Come on, funny girl!’ Don said. ‘Let’s all hear the joke.’

‘I was just thinking maybe you ought to put some pants on. What if it’s some old dear who’s run out of petrol?’

‘It’ll serve her right. Waking folk up in the middle of the night. And when they’re on holiday, too!’

Don swung the door open and peered out across the moonlit garden. Nothing moved. No sound broke the silence of the warm night.

‘Well?’ Terri asked impatiently, rising on her toes to look over his shoulder.

Don shrugged. ‘Nothing. Not a thing. You want to go out and check yourself?’

Terri stuck out her tongue. ‘Clever beggar.’

As Don turned to step back inside he placed his foot on something that made him yell out loud.

‘You have such a delicate turn of phrase,’ Terri said.

‘Jesus, it bloody well hurt!’ he growled. He raised his foot and explored the sole. Gave a harsh gasp as he drew a long, thick splinter of wood from the soft flesh. ‘Damn!’

‘Don . . . look!’

The note of urgency in Terri’s voice drew his attention. She was pointing at the open door.

The lower half of the door — which was made from solid, aged timber — bore fresh, deep gouges that bit deep into the wood. Don studied the marks, puzzled. He glanced about the immediate area. On the ground lay scattered splinters of wood, evidence of what had taken place.

Checking further away from the door Don noticed a series of scuff marks in the gravel path and some deeper impressions in the flowerbed edging the lawn.

'Don, come on back!' Terri called.

He joined her just inside the door and slipped an arm around her bare shoulders. She was trembling.

She smiled at him nervously. 'What could make marks like those in a thick wooden door?'

He shook his head. 'Haven't the faintest idea, love. Have to be something pretty big. A fox maybe.'

'I've never heard of a fox scratching at a door in the middle of the night. Or having the strength to claw deep gouges in it. I don't think a fox did that,' she added, pointing to the scarred wood. She stepped round Don and closed the door with a bang, locking and bolting it. 'In the morning we'll ring the police in Port Pendall. Let them look into it.'

'If it means we can get back to bed, love, I agree.'

They made their way back upstairs. Don switched off the light. In the darkness his feelings were concealed. Whatever had made those marks had been no fox. Accepting that meant it had to be something else. But what? The explanation could be very simple and straightforward. But that didn't make him feel any better.

* * *

'I'll look into it, Mr Ransome,' Trevor Parkinson said. He closed his notebook and slipped it into his back pocket.

'Any ideas?' Don asked. In the light of day the matter took on a less sinister aspect. 'We were thinking along the lines of a fox. But I suppose it could have been a hungry stray dog.'

'More likely to be a dog than a fox, sir,' Parkinson said. 'We haven't had many foxes around this area for years. Used to be a lot of hunting going on. They pretty well wiped out the local fox population.'

'Could a dog have made those marks in the door?' Terri asked.

'Hard to say, miss. Mind, it's surprising

how strong some dogs can be.'

'What about an escaped animal from a circus?'

'If something like that was on the loose, miss, we would have had some report. There is a circus playing over by Penzance but they haven't said anything about a missing animal.'

Terri shrugged, dismissing the thought. 'It was just an idea. I mean the marks are there. I heard the noise. Something did it. All that's missing now is just what it was.'

Parkinson smiled. 'I'll do some checking around. Missing animals and the like. There is another thought.'

'What's that?'

'Perhaps it wasn't an animal.'

Don frowned. 'Then what? Oh, I think I see what you're getting at. Maybe it was somebody's idea of a joke? To give us a scare?'

'Some people do have a weird sense of humour, sir.'

'We'll add it to the list,' Terri said.

'I'll keep in touch,' Parkinson said as he walked back to his car. 'If anything else happens let me know.'

'All right,' Don said. 'And thanks for coming.'

On the road back to town Trevor found himself thinking about Matt Trevo and his cold-store door. Unfortunately he didn't have any more time to devote to the matter. There were more pressing things to attend to. The day before a local girl had gone missing. Out for an early evening walk with her dog she had failed to return home. The dog had been found the next morning unharmed and tired. There was no trace of the girl at all. Not one single, hard fact pointing to the reason or cause for her disappearance. Family and friends and employers had all said the same thing. That Gillian Bampton had been a happy, settled girl with no apparent worries. Friendly and popular, Gillian had as secure a future as anyone could have. Of course, the police had hinted, there might be more to it than simply a girl vanishing completely of her own accord. Foul play could not be ruled out until proof showed otherwise. There was the possibility of Gillian having found herself a boyfriend and the pair of them having gone off together. It would have been completely out of character, Parkinson decided, but despite that fact it wasn't impossible. People *were* capable completely altering their lifestyle. Doing things they might never have contemplated at an earlier time in their lives. Parkinson sighed, resigned to the fact that it was just another avenue requiring investigation. And that meant more enquiries. More paperwork. More . . . He swore under his breath, then grinned at his reflection in the car's windscreen. Wasn't that the reason he'd joined the force? The excitement. The challenge. Like hell it was! He was still smiling as he drew up outside Port Pendall's police station.

It was even hotter inside the building than out on the street. The station was a relic. A throwback to the days when the local bobby did his rounds on a bike and the telephone had only just been invented. The building had thick walls and high, vaulted ceilings. Its windows were set way up off the floor and hadn't been opened since the turn of the century. Parkinson made his way along to the station sergeant's counter, his shoes rattling loudly on the stone floor of the passage.

'Parkinson!'

That was Sergeant Gifford. It was rumoured that Gifford had been born a copper. In fact it was a standing joke that when the doctor had held up the newborn baby, Gifford had been clutching his truncheon in his hand. Parkinson could believe it. Calling Gifford a bastard was being nice to the man.

'Yes, Sarge?'

'Where've you been?' Gifford asked. He was peering across the polished top of the counter, his usually red face practically glowing from the heat.

'Up to Cove Cottage, Sarge,' Parkinson said. 'Couple staying there on holiday had a scare last night. Heard noises and found scratches in the door.'

'And what did we assume had done it, then?' Gifford asked dryly. 'Werewolves?'

'No, Sarge. Wasn't a full moon last night,' Parkinson replied sharply, and then mentally kicked himself.

Gifford's bushy eyebrows lifted fractionally. 'Feeling smart today, are we? All right, Constable Parkinson, climb back into your Noddy car and get up to High Moor. Inspector Braddock wants it checked from end to end.'

'What am I looking for?'

'One missing girl. Name of Gillian Bampton.'

'That could take a couple of days, Sarge,' Parkinson protested.

Gifford's smile was almost apologetic. 'At *least* a couple of days!'

'Sarge, I've got reports to write up.'

'They'll have to wait, my lad.'

'Have a heart, Sarge.'

'Come, come, now, Constable Parkinson, surely you've heard? I never had one when I was born! Now move, my lad, and at the double!'

* * *

High Moor lay to the south of Port Pendall, extending for over ten miles in an easterly direction, nudging the rugged coastline in places. It was a wild and empty tract of land. Flat in areas, but given to undulating hills in others. There were shallow valleys and deep holes hidden by the thick bracken and dense brush. It was a place used mainly by the local farmers who ran their flocks of sheep across the silent slopes. Sometimes experienced walkers would cross it, though they did so aware of the pitfalls. Mist, drifting in from the sea, could blanket the moor quickly, obscuring the sunlight and concealing every landmark for miles around. High Moor presented nature in its best and worst moods — beautiful and treacherous.

Trevor Parkinson pulled the Panda car off the road and climbed out, wincing as the hot sun burned through his shirt. He stared out across the rolling expanse of moorland, seeing the heat-waves shimmering in the still air, and muttered softly to himself.

Gifford was bloody daft! How could one man be expected to search an area like this all on his own? It was impossible. He shoved his cap to the back of his head and snatched up the heavy binoculars from the car seat. He spent the next ten minutes slowly and carefully examining sections of the moor through the powerful glasses. He saw nothing except the thick undergrowth and a few sheep. He finally lowered the glasses. *This was a waste of time*! The proper way to search High Moor was with an organised party of men.

The car radio burst into life. Parkinson acknowledged the call and was instructed to break off his present assignment and drive a few miles along the coast road to Trenchard's Cove, part of High Moor named after a local smuggler of the last century, and a popular picnic area.

When he arrived Parkinson found a noisy group of people gathered round a crying woman who was being comforted by a dark-haired, stocky man wearing baggy shorts and a shirt that would have been more at home on the beach at Honolulu.

'Police 'ave arrived!' someone declared loudly.

Heads turned as Parkinson approached.

'It's her little girl who's gone missing.

Poor little thing. Gone and got herself lost. Here one minute and then she just seemed to vanish.'

Parkinson took out his notebook and turned to the parents, thinking idly that this was getting to be a habit.

4

'There it is,' Eddie Machin said, a satisfied smirk creasing his unshaven face. 'I told you he'd be there, didn't I?'

Jock Finerty nodded grudgingly. 'All right! Don't go on! You're worse than a bleedin' old woman!'

Eddie, still grinning, slipped out from the cover of the trees, with Jock close behind. They quickly crossed the shadowed road, making for the parked single-decker coach that was pulled in against the grass banking of the dark layby.

The coach was a familiar sight in the area. The owner, Harry Butlin, had converted it into a mobile snack bar. During the holiday season he ran the coach up and down the coast road selling quick meals, sandwiches, and hot and cold drinks. There were even a few tables inside where customers could sit and eat if they wished. Harry's coach was a popular attraction in the Port Pendall area and he did a steady trade during the season.

His day was a long one. He set out early and finished late. It was always after ten-thirty each night before he closed. And always, prior to driving home, he would park in this particular spot, count his takings for the day, and have a large mug of hot, sweet tea. Harry had carried out this ritual every evening for the past six years and this night was no different from any other — not until someone rapped on the locked door.

Harry glanced up from the newspaper he was reading. The knock was repeated. Harry grumbled under his breath as he got up and shuffled slowly towards the door.

'I'm closed,' he called out.

'Please, Mister, I need help! Had an accident with the car! I'm hurt!'

Harry sighed as he released the door's lock. He had been on his feet all day and really wanted nothing more than to finish his mug of tea so he could drive home. Still, he couldn't ignore a request for help.

As he was sliding the door open a thought flashed through his weary mind. Suppose it wasn't a genuine plea for help? What if it was a trick to get him to open the door? *You bloody fool, Harry!* He knew he should have made certain! He made a grab for the door handle . . .

Too late!

A large, grubby hand came round the edge of the door. Powerful fingers closed around Harry's wrist, twisting it cruelly. A heavy body clad in dirty denims filled the doorway. Harry, struggling to free himself, had a quick glimpse of a broad, unshaven face. Hard, bloodshot eyes. Lips peeling back from stained, rotted teeth. Matted dark hair reaching the collar of a greasy jacket.

A vicious blow struck Harry full in the chest. He crashed against the far side of the coach, gasping as savage pain engulfed his left shoulder. He felt something warm and wet trickle down his back. Ignoring the pain he made an attempt to regain his balance. He sensed movement close to him. Felt the front of his shirt being screwed up as rough hands grasped it.

'Don't . . . ' he pleaded.

His cry was ignored. A sharp burst of laughter preceded a powerful lunge that pulled Harry away from the wall and hurled him the length of the vehicle. His motion was brutally halted by the counter that spanned the width of the coach. There was a sickening crunch as Harry's face smashed down. Bright streamers of blood spidered out across the counter. Plates and cups, dislodged by the impact, showered to the floor. Harry cried out against the pain in his face. It exploded, swelling and expanding, then gelled into numbness. Harry became detached from reality, unable to control his actions and he slumped, blood dribbling freely from his damaged face.

Behind Eddie Machin the door closed with a bang.

'He going to give us any more trouble?' Jock Finerty asked as he relocked the door.

'No chance,' Eddie grinned. He stood over Harry Butlin's prostrate form, then without warning drew back one booted foot, smashing the tip against Harry's exposed side. The force of the blow twisted Harry round, drawing a long, low moan from his bloody lips.

Eddie moved away then, as if his mind had abruptly changed direction. He went around the end of the counter and began to search through the shelves.

'Come on, Jock, give us 'and! I want to find that fuckin' money an' get the hell out of 'ere!'

Between them the pair searched methodically, littering the floor with items that got in their way. Broken bottles spread their contents across the floor, speckled the sides of the coach.

'Sod this!' Jock yelled. 'Bloody waste of time!' He stalked across and bent over Harry's motionless form. He took hold of his hair, brutally yanking the man's head up off the floor. 'Listen to me, you old fart! You make up your mind which is more important to you! Your fuckin' health or your money!'

Harry stared up into his tormentor's face, realising with a cold chill that these two would cripple him without a second thought if the notion entered their

Neanderthal minds. He would regret losing the money — but better that than losing his life.

'Okay . . . okay . . . you can have the money!'

Jock grinned. He dragged Harry to his feet, thrusting him against the counter.

'Get it,' Eddie snapped. 'Quick!'

Stumbling, doubled over in agony, Harry made his painful way to the far end of the coach. Crouching, he lifted the small, square flap set in the floor, exposing a recessed box. In the box was a leather bag holding the day's takings; Harry had had a good day and the bag held over £300. He lifted the bag and handed it to Eddie Machin.

'Satisfied?' Harry asked, failing to keep the bitterness out of his voice.

The words were lost on both Eddie and Jock. They were pawing through the crumpled notes and gleaming coins. They had what they'd come for — Harry didn't interest them any longer; he realised this and stayed silently in the background, hoping that they would take the money and leave without bothering him again.

Which was exactly what they did. Without another look in Harry's direction the triumphant pair left. The moment they were through the door Harry staggered across, slammed it shut and locked it . . .

Neither Eddie nor Jock heard the door bang shut. Their thoughts were dominated by the money.

They ran directly into the shadowed closeness of the trees that edged the road. The timber spread away from them, moonlight shafting down through the canopy of intertwining foliage. The pale illumination broke up the denser shadows, leaving a weave of dark and light.

Eddie and Jock worked their way through the wood. It was only when they reached the far side that they paused in their hectic flight and panting for breath, bodies sticky with sweat, they flopped to the ground, staring up through the branches.

Eddie sat up abruptly, peering about him, a puzzled frown on his face.

'What's up?' Jock asked.

'It's too bloody quiet. Haven't you noticed?'

Jock raised his head. 'Always quiet at night, you pillock!'

'No it ain't,' Eddie insisted. 'There's always *some* kind of noise goin' on. I know the woods.'

'Daniel fuckin' Boone!' Jock giggled. 'Come on, let's have a look at that money.'

'Shurrup for a minute!' Eddie snapped. He thrust out a hand in warning, and Jock, knowing his companion's temper, kept his mouth closed.

For a while they sat in complete silence.

'Bloody told you,' Eddie commented finally.

'So what does it mean?'

Eddie shrugged. 'Don't know. But it ain't natural.'

Jock was about to pass some crude remark when he was startled by a sudden rattling in the undergrowth.

'Don't seem all that quiet to me!'

Eddie didn't reply.

Puzzled now by his partner's sudden reluctance to speak, Jock glanced across at him. Eddie was staring in his direction, though slightly to one side, over Jock's left shoulder.

'What you starin' at?'

Eddie began to stand up. Still staring, still silent.

'For fuck's sake, Eddie!'

Behind Jock the undergrowth cracked as something moved through it with considerable force. The sound filled the stillness and even Jock was forced to take notice. He sat upright, started to turn. The brittle rattle filled his ears, the sound rising, seeming to reach out for him.

'*Jesus Christ*!' Eddie yelled, his face stretched taut in an expression of utter disbelief and horror.

A nameless fear clutched at Jock's very being. Eddie's terror infected him and Jock uttered a shrill scream of his own. Still rising to his feet. Still turning. Knowing something was terribly wrong, yet unable to see what it was . . .

A crushing force closed around his neck. Jock felt flesh part. Felt muscle and tendon tear. Blood began to flow, warm and fluid, soaking into the fabric of his shirt. He panicked, struggled against the cruel bite encircling his neck. Reaching up he groped blindly, fingers touching hard, curving, bone-like shapes that were already slippery with his blood. His struggles increased. Body squirming, jerking, feet scrabbling against the soft earth, kicking up thick leafmould. A hoarse scream rose in his throat. The taste of blood spread across his swelling tongue. Fraction by fraction his breath was being cut off. His chest heaved. Eyes widened. The pressure on his neck increased. Became unbearable. Deep inside bone cracked. His jerking legs stilled. Thin runnels of blood wormed from his ears. Bubbled down his nose. His struggles lessened. Hands dropped to his sides. He was hardly aware of the sharp, needle-like object digging into his left side, just above the hip. Almost immediately a numbing warmth coursed through his body. The sensation akin to being immersed in deep, warm water. Jock's body seemed to drift, leaving him detached. Away from reality. His flesh not belonging to him any longer.

In the final seconds — before he slid

into an eternal darkness — Jock found his gaze centring on Eddie *and* the thing that was brutally tearing him apart. Shredding flesh from bone. Exposing living organs and severed arteries from which jets of blood pulsed. It was like some terrible dream. Something he was separate from yet also part of. A dark, evil nightmare. But he knew that it was no fantasy. Because the pain was real. And the writhing, bloody, pink and white thing that shrieked and sobbed had been his friend Eddie. And then, mercifully, the dark, silent night began to close in. Blotting out all sound and sight and feeling. Smothering him in a heavy, cloying blanket that pushed him deeper and deeper, down, down, until there was nothing.

Nothing . . .

5

'Come in, Parkinson, and close the door.'

Trevor Parkinson pushed the door to and crossed the office in quick, nervous strides.

'Sit down, lad,' Detective Inspector Sam Braddock said. 'Sergeant Gifford seems to think you're going to waste my time. Are you?'

'I hope not, sir.'

Braddock, a competent, young-looking forty-year-old, leaned back in his chair. He fixed his brown eyes on the young constable's face. 'I'm listening.'

A brown folder was held in Parkinson's hands. He placed it on the desk in front of him and opened it, removing a sheaf of papers which he spread out.

'I must point out, sir, that what I'm going to say is nothing more than speculation at this moment. Until I was able to sit down and start writing out these reports I hadn't been aware of certain similarities.'

Braddock peered across the desk at the neat row of report sheets before him. 'Go on,' he urged.

'These reports cover a number of incidents that go back over the last ten days. The first was an unusual break in at Trevo's butcher shop. A heavy wooden door on a meat-store literally torn open. Meat inside the store badly damaged. Then there was fencing badly damaged on the Needham farm, and some sheep missing. The next concerns a holiday home — Cove Cottage. Couple staying there reported receiving an unknown visitor in the early hours of the morning. All we found was structural damage. Other reports concern missing livestock up on High Moor. Altogether something like ten to twelve sheep have vanished. Also we have these missing people. First the Bampton girl. Then an eight-year-old child who disappeared up on the fringe of High Moor. The two tearaways who beat up and robbed Harry Butlin. All we found was the bag of money they'd taken. No sign of the two men. A few traces of a struggle in the woods where we picked up the money. Then there have been other complaints about odd noises at night. A few 'things' seen lurking behind bushes. Some could be genuine, but I do think there are a few brought on by too much to drink.'

There was a short silence after Parkinson finished speaking. Braddock, who had been staring fixedly at a point on the far wall, gathered up the reports and read through one or two.

'Just one question, Parkinson.'

'Sir?'

'What makes you think any of these incidents might be connected?'

'The similarity in the damage done at Trevo's butcher shop to that at the Needham farm and Cove Cottage.'

'Doesn't apply to the missing people — or do you think it does?'

'I'm sure all the events *are* related to one another,' Parkinson said, refusing to allow himself to be put off his stride. 'I'll admit that part of it is just a feeling, sir, but there's a link to tie them all together if we can find it.'

'Sounds like intuition,' Braddock observed.
'It is, sir.'
'Well hang onto that, Parkinson, because it's an asset. Intuition. Instinct. Gut feeling. Call it what you want. It's part of what goes to make a good copper. And I think you're right. Somewhere in amongst this little lot, unrelated on the surface, *is* a link. All we have to do is find it. Isolate it.' Braddock put down the reports. 'I've been impressed by the way you've followed this through, Parkinson, and I'd like you to carry on with it. Working with me. From today you're relieved of all other duties and placed on my squad. I'll have a word with Sergeant Gifford. He won't like me pinching one of his men, but I'll smooth things over. Now, have you got your own car?'
'Yes, sir.'
'All right. Take it and get off home. Change into plainclothes and report back here as quick as you can.'
'Yes, sir. Thank you, sir.'
Braddock nodded. 'Just make sure I haven't done the wrong thing, Parkinson. Fall down and you'll be back on your beat

faster than you can dial 999!'

'I won't let you down, sir.'

'Oh, just one thing,' Braddock said as Parkinson reached the door.

'Sir?'

'For Christ's sake resist the urge to look too damned pleased with yourself when you pass Gifford's desk. If he thinks you're giving him a mental vee sign even I won't be able to save you.'

'Yes, sir,' Parkinson said, edging through the door.

In the locker room in the basement he took off his uniform jacket. Placing it, along with his cap, in the locker he slipped on the light sports coat he wore when he was off duty. On his way to the station car park he had to pass Gifford's corner and even as he approached the long desk he could see the sergeant watching him.

'Going to slip into our best suit, are we?' Gifford asked dryly. 'A member of the *élite* now, Parkinson, so mind your manners. Just you take things easy, my lad, and always remember what befell poor Cinderella on the stroke of midnight!'

Trevor Parkinson drove to his flat, took a quick shower, dressed in civilian clothing, and returned to the station. He was given a small office next to Braddock's. It was bare except for a desk, two chairs, a filing cabinet and a telephone. In the middle of the desk was a thick file of papers. Parkinson took off his coat and sat down. He opened the first file, which contained every known thing about Gillian Bampton, and began to learn just what investigative police work was all about.

6

'Damn it, Don, there it is again!'

Terri Sheldon sat up, peering through the semi-darkness. Beside her Don Ransome grumbled, his naked body stirring restlessly.

'Don? Don?' Terri found she was reluctant to raise her voice above an urgent whisper. 'Oh, damn you!' she hissed, throwing aside the covers. Out of bed she crossed the room and eased open the door, making her way across the landing and down the stairs to the living-room.

Now she could hear the sound distinctly. Outside the front door. A heavy, insistent scratching. Exactly the same kind of noise she'd heard four nights ago. For a while she remained where she was. Just listening. A faint shiver of fear slithered along her spine and she felt cold despite the oppressive heat of the night.

Her curiosity eventually got the better of her and, overriding caution, she moved towards the front door, flicking on the light as she passed the switch.

It was the last decisive move she ever made . . .

The front door shattered. Panels and frame disintegrated under extreme pressure. Splinters of wood flew across the room, sharp edges gashing Terri's naked flesh. She raised her hands to protect her face, cringing against the stinging pain.

Scuffling sounds filled her ears. Coupled with a dry, sibilant hiss. Terri inhaled a cloying, musky scent that made her choke; a strange odour, unidentifiable yet repellantly intoxicating.

She lowered her hands from her eyes and her mind utterly rejected what she saw.

There were three mutated scorpions. In their eagerness to get through the doorway they had jammed their bodies into the opening and jostled angrily, legs scraping against the stone step. There was a moment of confusion, each scorpion determined to dominate the others. Then the sheer brute strength of the wriggling bodies catapulted them through the doorway and into the room.

In those fleeting seconds, Terri was still registering the scene on her mind. If she had been allowed a few seconds longer she would have made some attempt to run.

She was not accorded that opportunity.

The scorpions separated, scuttering across the floor, pincered arms held before them. The long tails curved up and over the dark, flexible bodies.

One — a shade swifter than its companions — extended one arm in a short arc, the powerful pincers savagely ripping a foot-long gash across Terri's left hip. Lacerated flesh hung in tatters. Blood streamed from the raw, pulpy wound. Beads of spilled blood spattered the scorpion's shell as it made a similar thrust with its other arm. The sharp tips of the pincer penetrated with ease. And an awful scream burst from Terri's throat as they drove deep into her body. The claws encountered curving rib bones, then retracted in an eruption of blood and splintered rib bone.

The other scorpions darted forward and in a hideous frenzy of mutilation, they dragged the girl to the floor, repeatedly sinking their glistening stings into the unprotected flesh.

One of the scorpions abruptly moved away from its companions, scuttling to the foot of the stairs as its sensors picked up movement.

Don Ransome, groggy from sleep, slowly descended the stairs. He'd been aware of Terri climbing out of bed and leaving the room, but had only registered her disappearance fully when the loud crack of splintering wood had reached him. By the time he had made his way to the stairs, Terri Sheldon was already beyond help.

Now, blinking his eyes against the light, Don stared — horrified — at the grisly scene before him.

Terri lay on the living-room floor, her blood-streaked body ripped and mutilated beyond recognition. Hovering close by were two huge, insect-like creatures, their black bodies wet with blood.

'Get away from her!' Don was enraged. Totally unconcerned for his own safety, he continued down the stairs, still yelling.

He failed to see the third scorpion. It had held itself motionless near the bottom of the stairs. Waiting . . .

Don heard the scuffling at the last moment. He caught a glimpse of something long and dark emerging from the shadows below him.

Too late he saw the danger. Attempted to draw back.

The advancing scorpion extended an arm, closing the pincer around Don's left leg just below the knee. With seemingly little effort the pincer sheared through bone; the crack drowned by Don's shriek of agony. Helpless, he felt himself dragged forward, down the stairs. His wild struggles were futile. The scorpion tugged effortlessly, tipping him off balance and Don pitched forward. He crashed to the floor his face crushed against the hard boards. Blood oozed from his broken nose.

As he numbly registered the need to climb to his feet, a heavy, squirming weight landed on his back, spiny legs scrabbling for a grip. Don reacted instinctively, his body attempting to reject the alien thing in contact with it. Twisting, writhing, screaming, his mind sick with horror, Don fought a brief, hopeless struggle for his life.

Brutal pincers hooked beneath his jaw, drawing his head back until the skin of his throat was pulled taut. He felt his muscles popping with tension. Knew that unless some kind of miracle manifested itself within the next few seconds he was going to die; he fought during those final moments, hands groping blindly, senses recoiling from contact with the shell-hard body. For a brief moment his fingers found a hold, gripped fiercely — and then the scorpion's tail curved over its head, the long, tapering sting sinking into the exposed throat, injecting a stream of deadly venom. Don's body arched violently, feet drummed against the bloodied floorboards, and then relaxed.

The scorpions gathered around the still bodies, deliberating for a time before dragging them out of the cottage and into the darkness beyond.

* * *

As Braddock's car drew to a halt outside Cove Cottage he was already pushing open his door. Nodding to the uniformed constable at the gate, Braddock walked down the path. Before he reached the front entrance Trevor Parkinson appeared and came to meet him.

'Well?' Braddock asked.

Parkinson shook his head. 'We've searched the immediate area, sir. No sign of the bodies.'

'Damn!'

Parkinson led the way inside. 'This is how I found the place when I arrived earlier.'

Braddock took in the scene before him. The living-room floor littered with shattered fragments of the door, pooled with congealing blood. There were splashes of it across the wall near the stairs.

'The two people — you think they were here last night?'

'Yes, sir. I checked the bedroom. Clothes on bedside chairs. A man's watch and wallet, loose change on the dresser. Woman's handbag. Make-up. Not the kind of things usually left behind if someone leaves a house under normal circumstances.'

Braddock took out a pack of slim cigars and lit one. He wandered around the room, his eyes searching.

'Have you informed the forensic boys?'

Parkinson nodded. 'They're sending a team from Penzance, sir.'

'Good.' Braddock sighed. 'All right, Parkinson. For now have the search extended. Cover as much ground as possible. Trouble is there's a lot of rough country in this area. Not the easiest to search. But we've got to go through the motions.'

'I don't think we'll find anything, sir.'

'Intuition again, Parkinson?'

'Just a feeling, sir.'

'You must get 'em from the same place I do. I'm going back to the office. As soon as you've set up the search I want you back there as well.'

'Yes, sir.'

'If the local press gets onto this don't say anything. No theories. No anything. I don't want any panic stories in the papers. We keep a low profile on this until we get some idea what we're dealing with.'

'I wonder just *what* it is, sir.'

'That, Parkinson, is well and truly open to speculation.'

7

The pub had whitewashed walls and a thatched roof. Inside it sported *real* oak beams that were hung with pewter tankards and faded photographs old at the turn of the century. The pub was called The Guillemot and it was in every sense of the word a local, catering for the farmworkers and tradespeople living in the area. It sold a locally brewed cider that came in aged wood casks, and the grizzled elders who occupied the smooth-worn benches in the bar would have snorted with contempt if anyone had tried to introduce beer in ringpull cans.

Very few tourists used the place. It was too small to cater for crowds anyway. Nor did it pander to the trendy fads of other pubs; there were no pounding juke-boxes or electronic games; a total lack of 'pub food'. The Guillemot provided the basic function of the pub — a tranquil place where friends could meet for good conversation and an equally good drink.

The cool interior belied the heat of the day beyond the thick walls of weathered stone. A subdued murmur of voices mingled with the clink of glasses. Above the nodding heads of the dozen or so patrons hung a thick layer of tobacco smoke. Behind the bar the landlord slowly and leisurely wiped dry the glasses he'd just rinsed. He glanced at the clock on the wall behind him, noting that there were five minutes until closing. Then he would spend half an hour clearing away before he sat down to his lunch.

'Fill 'er up, Barney.'

Barney Daley took the pint glass that had been firmly placed on the polished bar top and refilled it. He pushed the foam-topped glass in the direction of the sun-browned, white-haired old man waiting for it.

'Get it down, Tommy,' Barney said. He jabbed a finger in the direction of the clock. 'Be closing time in a few minutes.'

Tommy picked up the glass in a gnarled hand. 'That's your one fault, young Daley,' he grumbled. 'You're always in a hurry. Time you learned life's too short for bein' too hasty.'

A wry smile edged Barney Daley's lips. Tommy, who was close on eighty-five himself, always insisted on calling the pub's landlord *young* Daley — even though Barney was fifty-six-years-old.

'Here, I haven't . . . 'Tommy began on some topic important enough to generate speech; whatever it was remained in a vocal limbo as the pub's double doors were flung open, the glass panels shattering against the inner walls.

'What the hell is going on?' Barney Daley yelled.

A man lurched into the pub. He stumbled; collided with a table, sending glasses flying across the bar room. He reached out to steady himself against the wall and his hand dripped blood, leaving a long red smear along the painted surface. Blood masked most of his face too, oozing freely from deep, raw gouges that started somewhere above his hairline and terminated at his throat, it was as if powerful claws had raked the entire head, peeling off sections of hair and scalp, practically severing the left ear and laying open the cheek. The hideous wounds were not confined to the head. The man's shirt hung in bloody tatters, exposing his lacerated chest and gouged stomach. The right arm hung limply at his side, a sodden mass; the upper limb virtually devoid of flesh, showing a knotted bulge of muscle and tendons dangling loosely.

The patrons of the pub stared at the newcomer in stunned silence. He gazed around him, eyes searching, dull with pain, and mirroring the still fresh memory of some unspeakable horror.

A glass — knocked over on its side — rolled off the edge of a table and shattered as it hit the floor. The sound broke the silence and the paralysis.

'What's happened, man?' Barney Daley asked, coming quickly round the bar.

As the landlord neared him the man took a faltering step forward and plunged to the floor. As he fell he brushed his hand against the front of Barney's shirt, leaving a large bloodstain. Bending over him Barney searched for a pulse. He straightened and went to the bar, pulling out the telephone he kept near the till. Dialling quickly he made contact with the Port Pendall police and told them what had happened.

* * *

Doctor Richard Groves finished scrubbing his hands, rinsed and dried them, and then made his way to his office. He switched on the desk-light and sat down, glancing at his watch, seeing with some surprise that it was almost nine-thirty. He leaned back in his seat, deep in thought. Finally he sat forward, picking up the printed sheets that rested there. He studied the paper, his tired eyes finding it difficult to focus on the words.

Reaching across the desk he drew the telephone to him. He dialled the operator and waited impatiently, speaking briefly when she answered. There was another delay before the operator came back on the line with the information Groves wanted. Breaking the connection he dialled the number he'd been given. He listened to the ringing-tone for a long time before the receiver was lifted and a man's voice answered.

'Am I speaking to Miles Ranleigh the entomologist?' Groves asked.

'Yes. Who's this?'

'I am Richard Groves, Mr Ranleigh. I'm calling from my office at the Port Pendall Hospital in Cornwall. First I want to apologise for ringing so late . . .'

'Don't worry about that,' Ranleigh said. 'From the tone of your voice I'd say you have something important on your mind.'

'I think this matter could be extremely important, Mr Ranleigh. Important enough for me to suggest that you travel down to Port Pendall as soon as possible.'

'Can you explain why?'

'I've just completed an autopsy on a man who was brought in this afternoon and who died a couple of hours later. The post mortem revealed that, apart from the severe physical damage done to him, his death was brought about by the unbelievably large amount of toxic venom in his body. I ran some lab analysis tests on blood samples and the result staggered me, Mr Ranleigh. You see, I read the paper you wrote concerning those mutated scorpions in Kent. While I was carrying out the post mortem I began to think about your paper. So I located it and re-read it. When I checked my lab break-down of the venom against your results in the paper I realised my intuition had not let me down. Both venoms were the same, apart from the fact that the sample I have is far more powerful.'

Miles Ranleigh didn't respond immediately. When he did, his words were deliberately precise. 'Groves, during your examination of the body did you find anything which might possibly be described as a puncture mark — the kind resulting from a sting of some kind?'

'I was coming to that and something else. Yes, I did find such a mark. At the base of the neck. Just below the hairline. It wasn't easily noticeable. That was the other thing I wanted to tell you. The whole of the skin area — the entire body — has turned black. Again the same kind of reaction experienced by the victims of the Long Point scorpions.'

‘Anything else?’

‘Just one observation. The size of the puncture. It’s far larger than anything one might expect from a creature the size of a scorpion.’ Groves paused. ‘Mr Ranleigh, I could be completely wrong about all this. Possibly I’m reading something into the death of this man which isn’t really there. Just relating his condition to those in your paper and assuming they’re the same.’

‘Doctor, you say you’ve read my paper?’

‘Yes.’

‘Then you will have taken account of the number of deaths brought about by the scorpions during the Long Point incident. I don’t think we can be too careful if there’s a possibility of a similar threat recurring. I think your suggestion is sound. I’ll leave as soon as I’ve thrown a few things in a bag.’

8

Andy Lloyd switched off his powerful flashlight, satisfied that it wouldn't let him down, and turned to check if his companion was also ready.

'All set,' Pete Crawford said.

Andy nodded and led the way down the short slope and into the shadowed entrance of the main tunnel of the long-inactive Pendall and High Moor Tin Mine. In the late 1800s and early 1900s the Cornish mining industry had been at its peak, but the availability of cheaper material from other countries gradually forced the Cornish mines out of business. Added to the competition the Pendall mine found itself threatened by dwindling ore seams. Although it was believed that there was more to be found, a further complication arose in the form of water seepage in the lower levels of the main tunnel. At first it was thought it was the sea working its way through because the main shaft went out under the water. This was found to be wrong. The water was fresh. Drillings were taken and it was realised that behind the rock face was some vast underground watercourse; a subterranean river. Only the rock face held it back. Contained the terrifying power of all those tons of water just waiting to burst free. Along with many others the Pendall mine lay deserted for decades. Then there was talk of starting them up again. The mines at Pendeen and the South Crofty Mine at Illogan were reopened and this stirred interest in the Pendall mine. An investigation into the possibility took place. Andy Lloyd and Pete Crawford, both Cornish, studying Mine Engineering, decided to take on the job of making a feasibility study of the Pendall mine as their summer break project.

Within yards of entering the tunnel Andy Lloyd found it necessary to switch on his flashlight. Pete did the same.

'We'd better stay pretty close,' Andy suggested. 'Keep the lights on the ground. I don't fancy falling down some damn great hole. The tunnel floor will start to slope down pretty steeply, too.'

'How deep do we go?' Pete asked.

'By the time we reach the furthest chamber we'll have dropped a couple of hundred feet.'

'Mmmm.' Pete shone his torch over the walls. 'Looks pretty sound here.'

'The faults will start to show deeper down.'

They moved along the shadowed tunnel, torches cutting through the greyness. The floor was littered with loose shale that rattled underfoot. Here and there water lay in hollows and the walls gleamed where it had seeped through the rock.

After a five minute walk, during which time they became aware of the tunnel's downward trend, they reached a gallery cut from the solid rock. From here a number of smaller tunnels angled deeper into the earth.

'According to those old maps, the centre tunnel is the main one. The others were only minor ones. The main one is the one extending out under the sea.'

Pete took the lead as they entered the tunnel. Again they were aware of the downward slope. After about a quarter mile they stopped.

'Looks pretty fair, even here,' Pete said. 'Few rock faults.'

'Not bad when you think it's been abandoned for close on a century. These timber supports are still solid. Roof's not too bad.' Andy shone his torch at the floor. 'Little more water seepage down here but I'd expect it at this level.' He dipped a finger in the water and tasted it. 'Fresh,' he said. 'Fresh water.'

'Yeah,' Pete said. He sleeved sweat off his face. 'Tell you what — there's a bloody awful smell.'

Andy sniffed, then wrinkled his nose. 'Christ, you're right.'

'What does it remind you of?'

'Rotten meat?'

'Just what I thought.'

They walked on, flashlights casting back and forth, crisscrossing as they probed the darkness.

'Could be some animal that got itself

lost. Sheep or something, I suppose,' Andy said.

'Hold on.' Pete reached out to touch Andy's shirt.

'Now what . . . ?' Andy began.

'Listen!'

Something clicked in the darkness ahead of them. Like a stone disturbed by a careless foot.

'Maybe we're not the only ones down here,' Pete remarked.

'Long way to bring your girlfriend for a quick one,' Andy grinned.

'Funny! Is sex all you ever think about?'

'Course not. Lot of the time I think about women.'

They heard the noise again, reaching along the confines of the tunnel. Echoing softly. This time it was closer.

'Hey! Anybody there?' Andy yelled. His words raced ahead, rolling off the rough-hewn walls, then drifting back as a fading echo.

Now the brittle clicking came again, this time becoming louder and louder with each passing moment.

‘Pete — what the hell is it?’

‘I’m not sure I want to find out,’ Pete said.

‘Oh come on!’ Andy grinned, his expression hiding his doubts. ‘It can’t be anything . . . ’

A wriggling shape erupted from the darkness, moving directly into the beam of Andy’s flashlight. He formed an indistinct picture of a long body supported on many legs — a pair of cold eyes reflecting the light from his torch. There was no more time to see anything else because the creature came straight for him, lunging forward and up.

Andy screamed as the scissoring pincers of the scorpion ripped through his clothing and into his flesh. His senses were repelled by the alien touch. His nostrils filled by the musky smell issuing from its body. As pain flared, hot and deep, he fell back against the rock wall and slid sideways, the wriggling body weighing him down, scaly legs gripping him. A tearing sensation just above his left hip was followed by a drenching wash of warm blood. He felt it soak his trousers, trickle thickly down his groin. The scorpion sank its other set of pincers into his chest, the edges cutting easily through muscle and bone. Andy struck out wildly, the heavy torch in his hand bouncing off the shell-hard body. The impact jarred it from Andy's fingers and it struck the floor, throwing its powerful beam of light along the dark tunnel.

For a frozen moment that might have been torn from some feverish nightmare, Andy Lloyd's gaze centred on the circle of light, and he saw a rippling flood of jostling scorpions moving along the tunnel. The hard light bounced off shining bodies and scuttling legs. Flexing arms tipped by cruel pincers. Grotesque shadows were flung against the walls; shadows that surged as the living flood rolled on — closing in on *him*.

Andy Lloyd had time for a final scream — a pitiful sound that briefly rose above the scuttering of the advancing horror — before he was overwhelmed, his twitching form vanishing beneath a smother of scorpions who fought between themselves in their eagerness to begin the hideous orgy of mutilation . . .

It was only as his companion vanished from sight that Pete Crawford moved himself, turning in one frenzied moment to run headlong down the tunnel. There was no thought for his friend. No concern — except for his own survival. To be able to return to the bright, open spaces above ground, away from this awful shadow world and the nightmare creatures it had spawned.

The bouncing beam of his torch cut a strong shaft of light through the darkness, jerking wildly from side to side as he ran. Stumbling. Loose footed. Uncoordinated. Falling. Skin tearing from the palm of his hand as he caught it against the rough stone. Somehow he managed to keep a grip on the torch. Scrambling upright he ran on, his lungs starting to burn, sweat slick on his body beneath his clinging clothes.

Ahead of him twin pinpoints of light appeared, close to the floor. They appeared to move rapidly forward.

Pete stopped running. He pressed hard against the rough wall. Desperately tried to slow the rapid heaving of his chest as his air-starved lungs fought back. He swung the beam of the torch along the tunnel, again picking up the reflected glow of light — and then saw the wriggling shape behind the light.

Another scorpion. Moving in his direction. High on stiffened legs. Tail curving up and over the arched body. Others behind it. He brought the torch round, shining it back the way he'd come and saw that the tunnel was jammed with jostling bodies.

There was no way out. He sagged back against the rock. He felt sick. Cold. His spine crawling with horror as he thought what those loathsome creatures would do to him. He switched off the torch, welcoming the darkness. He slid down the rough stone until he was sitting on the floor. A shudder coursed through his body and he wrapped his arms around himself, pressing his face into them. Now he could hear the sound of their approach. Dry, rustling whispers that drifted closer. Then harsher scraping as if something was being dragged along. A strange, musty smell filled his nostrils making him think of shaded hollows hidden deep in woods where decay and dead wild animals rotted beneath hot summer suns. He drew himself into a tight ball, knowing they were all around him. Hearing them yet blind to their presence. He wished himself so small they might overlook him. There was a violent thumping in his chest — his racing heart — and a coiled sickness in his stomach. Suddenly he felt a spreading wetness between his thighs; realisation of what he'd done filled him with shame and he felt tears sting his eyes.

Out of the darkness something reached and touched him. Something hard and curved. Something that opened and closed with measured deliberation. It slid across his left arm. Exploring, hesitating, then moving on. When it touched his wrist it paused . . . then drew away for an instant before returning, and this time there was no hesitation. Simply a powerful downward slash. Razor edges biting through flesh, severing tendons and drawing a sudden rush of blood. Pain followed instantly

— burning, awful pain that numbed his nervous system. In the few moments prior to a concentrated assault Pete Crawford did the only thing left open to him. He began to scream. The sound rising from the very depths of his tormented soul.

He screamed and he kept on screaming . . . not knowing that his last cry for help went unheard.

9

'I hate having to admit it but I don't think there's any doubt!'

Miles Ranleigh straightened up and turned away from the blackened corpse. He sighed as he crossed to where Richard Groves stood by a long lab bench. Ranleigh tapped a small glass phial.

'Your analysis of the blood sample is correct, too. The venom in it is identical to that found in the Long Point scorpions.'

'But of a much stronger toxicity.'

'This was the one thing we were concerned about during the Long Point affair. The possibility of any eggs being laid that might produce an advanced mutation.'

'Advanced how? Larger? More powerful?'

'We knew they could be larger after the discovery of the crippled scorpions in the first nest.'

'That was in the underground chamber? Where the radiation leak took place?'

Ranleigh nodded. 'The first large ones were destroyed — but the fear was that similar ones might be hatched from future eggs.'

'If all this proves true then there's the chance we might have some of these things in this area?'

Ranleigh shrugged. 'The possibility does exist.'

'Shall we go to my office?' Groves said and led the way.

They sat down. Groves leaned back in his seat. It was almost ten-thirty in the morning and the long night was catching up on him; he hadn't left the hospital since calling Ranleigh the night before. The entomologist had arrived a half-hour ago, having driven down from his home in Buckinghamshire, and had insisted on going straight in to look at the body.

'I know it's academic now — but how could the scorpions end up in Cornwall?'

'Any number of ways,' Ranleigh said. 'In a car or truck. They may have travelled in someone's luggage. And don't forget we're on the coast. They could have been on a boat.' He smiled wryly. 'It was the way their ancestors arrived in this country originally.'

'You talked about large scorpions, Mr Ranleigh. Just how large?'

'The ones found in the original nest at Long Point were in the region of two to three feet in length. I only saw photographs myself, but they looked pretty formidable. And despite being sick and crippled one of them managed to attack *and* kill a man. If my theory is correct and a second generation has evolved then we could be talking about fully-developed scorpions. They'd be pretty strong. As an example consider the wounds on that corpse.'

'I wish I could stop thinking about them,' Groves said.

'Oh, just one thing. Forget the Mr — the name's Miles.'

'All right, Miles; where do we go from here?'

'Until we know for certain just what we're up against I suggest we keep this to ourselves. Give me a chance to do a little scouting around. See if I can locate a nest. There has to be one somewhere.'

'Where would they locate it?'

'Below ground. Somewhere dark.'

Groves thought about Ranleigh's remark for a moment, then got to his feet and went to his filing cabinet. He took out a map which he unfolded and laid across the top of his desk.

'This is Port Pendall and the surrounding area. This is called High Moor. A young child vanished up *there* recently. Then a local girl disappeared while out walking her pet dog one evening. She lived *here*, at the opposite end of High Moor. On the fringe really. Closer to town. Apparently there have been a number of odd incidents over the past few weeks. Missing livestock. Damage to property. The police called me in to have a look at a holiday cottage after the couple in it had vanished one night. Place was in a hell of a mess. There was blood everywhere. I took samples and checked it. Turned out to be human blood. I also found traces of human flesh.'

'I haven't heard any mention of

anything in the papers or on TV.'

'The police are still searching for answers. Until they know just what's going on they decided to keep quiet.'

'Who's dealing with it?'

'A good man. Name of Sam Braddock.'

'Not the sort to throw a fit if I walk in and tell him he's got a possible invasion by four-foot scorpions brewing up?'

'*Sam Braddock*? No. He'll listen and then he'll act. Do you want to meet him?'

'Not yet,' Miles said. 'I want to have a look round first. Establish some facts.'

'Is there anything I can do?'

'Not right at this moment. I would appreciate it if you kept all we've said to yourself until there's a definite case to present.'

'Whatever you say.'

'Could I borrow that map?'

Groves folded the map and handed it to Miles. 'I have a list here detailing the places where there have been disappearances and the like. It might help.'

Miles took the list and folded it away with the map.

'I'll be in touch,' he said.

* * *

Miles Ranleigh drove a year-old Range Rover that had been repainted and fitted out with extras to his specifications. It was his one concession to personal indulgence, and as far as he was concerned it had been worth every penny. He drove away from the hospital, down to and through the crowded town of Port Pendall, regretting that he didn't have time to enjoy the weather, and followed the road that took him in the general direction of High Moor.

He spotted a roadside restaurant a couple of miles outside the town and pulled into the car park. Inside the bright, clean restaurant he chose a window table, ordered a late breakfast and coffee. Over his meal he checked the list Groves had given him against the map, marking each place. Before he'd completed the list he had become aware of an emerging pattern.

The various incidents all fell within a rough circle, the centre of which was the High Moor area. According to the list the most recent incidents were the ones on the outer edges of the circle. It was a widening pattern. Each incident a little further out from the centre than the previous one. Miles studied the map closely, a faint smile gradually touching his lips. He abruptly jabbed the map with a finger, causing his coffee cup to rattle loudly.

'*That's got to be it!*' he said to himself.

He was staring at the place indicated on the map by the legend: *Port Pendall and High Moor Tin Mine*. An abandoned mine! Of course. Underground. Long dark tunnels meandering beneath the earth. Just the kind of environment the scorpions would choose. Ideal for their nests. Their breeding ground. It was all beginning to fall into place. The trouble was if his assumption turned out to be correct, then Port Pendall's problems had only just begun.

Back on the road Miles followed the route he'd worked out on the map. It took a good half-hour to reach his destination. He guided the Range Rover off the road and across a stretch of rough ground. Off to his right, less than a quarter of a mile away, he caught the odd glimpse of blue water. He followed a faint, rutted track, mostly overgrown with grass and weeds, often obliterated completely. The track ended abruptly in a shallow basin with a high, sheer rockface blocking the way. At the foot of the rockface, practically overgrown with tangled undergrowth, Miles finally identified the dark outline of a tunnel mouth.

He walked slowly down the grassy slope towards the tunnel. His eyes scanned the ground and as he neared the mouth of the tunnel he noticed the deep marks scoring the grass and the earth beneath. They were similar to the ones reported outside Cove Cottage and at the Needham farm. No one had known the cause. Miles Ranleigh knew what had made them.

He stared at the dark tunnel mouth, shoulders hunched, his hands pushed deep into his jacket pockets. He had to be sure. Certain of his facts before he involved the police and set in motion any kind of defensive action. *He had to know!*

And that meant going into those underground tunnels to have a look. The thought scared him. Repelled him. But it had to be done. First, though, he was going to need certain special items of equipment. Miles turned away from the tunnel and started back towards the Range Rover.

And found himself face to face with an extremely attractive young woman.

She was tall and tanned, with a mass of black hair cut in one of those styles that appeared both casual *and* well-cared-for at the same time. She was dressed in comfortable, faded denims and a thin cotton shirt, which were probably more expensive than they looked. Noticing the slim but developed figure Miles decided that the money had been a good investment. Her clothes revealed and flattered her natural beauty without being over obvious.

'Did I startle you?' she asked.

Miles grinned. 'No. I get so wrapped up in what I'm doing I just don't notice people.'

'Yes, I know what you mean.'

As he stood beside her Miles caught a whiff of perfume, and he found himself glancing sideways at the girl. It was difficult not to. She *was* very lovely, and Miles Ranleigh didn't devote his entire life to the study of insects.

'Did you come to explore the mine?' she asked.

'No . . . not exactly.'

The girl glanced at him, frowning slightly.

'Are you . . . looking for someone?'

It was Miles's turn to stare. 'Should I be?'

A warning bell was sounding at the back of his mind, though the girl's question could easily have been nothing more than an innocent remark.

'Oh, I just wondered,' the girl went on. 'To be honest I'm not sure why I'm here myself. Only I . . . '

'Go on.'

She laughed nervously. 'I'm probably worrying over nothing.'

Miles bit back his impatience. 'Let me be the judge of that. Just tell me why you're here.'

‘The day before yesterday I was here and I met a couple of students. They were on their way to the mine to carry out some kind of survey.’

‘And they went in?’

‘I suppose so,’ the girl said. ‘I left them before we reached the mine, so I didn’t actually see them enter.’

‘But you think they did?’

She nodded.

‘What brought you back?’

‘I heard a small item on the local radio this morning. It was a request for information on the whereabouts of two young students. They are on holiday in the area but haven’t been heard from in the last couple of days. I suppose I just connected them together. The more I thought about it the more I convinced myself there might be something to worry about. You hear so many reports about people going down old tunnels and the like. I began to wonder if perhaps those two young men were down there somewhere. Trapped maybe. Hurt. But now I’m here it makes me realise that I could be over-reacting.’

'I don't think you are.'

'I knew you weren't just sightseeing,' the girl said. She stared at Miles. 'Your face is familiar. I'm pretty good on faces. Wait a minute. You were on a number of television reports. Oh, it must be over a year ago now.' She smiled in triumph. 'Miles Ranleigh. Am I right?'

'Yes.'

'It's the beard that gave you away. I always remember beards because I have a thing for them.'

'Gets them every time,' Miles remarked.

'Now — you were interviewed a number of times after that insect scare down in Kent. Something to do with scorpions, wasn't it?'

Miles nodded quickly. 'It was then,' he said. *Damn*, he thought. If he wasn't careful this astute young woman was going to start adding things up.

'So what is so interesting to an entomologist in an old, abandoned tin mine in Cornwall?'

Miles didn't answer, and regretted not doing so, because the silence hung heavily between them.

‘Lord, don’t tell me you’ve found more scorpions!’

Miles raised his hand. ‘There are a thousand reasons why I should be interested in old tin mines. And they don’t have to be related to entomology. Nor to an event which took place some time ago at the other end of the country.’

‘I’m beginning to think they might just be related to entomology *and* to scorpions, Mr Ranleigh. Whatever else you are, a good liar isn’t one of them.’

‘Can we talk?’ Miles asked. ‘Not here. Somewhere a bit less conspicuous.’

‘Of course.’ The girl indicated the Range Rover. ‘Take me for a drive in that fancy looking motor. That should be private enough.’

Miles opened the passenger door and the girl climbed in.

‘By the way, my name is Jill Ansty,’ she said.

As he walked around to his door Miles glanced in the direction of the tunnel entrance and despite the heat of the sun he shivered. Settling in his seat he switched on the engine and turned the

Range Rover round, driving back to the road.

'Do you live close by?' he asked.

Jill nodded. 'I'm borrowing a friend's cottage for a few weeks. It's a mile or so along the road.'

Miles cruised steadily along the narrow road, occasionally having to pull over against the grass verge to allow approaching traffic room to pass.

'Now, Mr Ranleigh, let's talk,' Jill said finally.

'I'd like whatever we say to remain between us for the moment,' Miles said. 'I'm not an alarmist but I do believe in calling a fact a fact.'

'And in this case?'

'It is probable — though not fully proved one way or the other — that there *are* specimens of mutated scorpions in this area.'

'How many? How did they get here?' Jill twisted round in her seat. 'Does anyone know?'

'Hey — slow down!' Miles said. 'I'll answer your last question first, because right now it's important. As far as I know, only three people at the moment. I'm one. A doctor at the local hospital, incidentally the man who alerted me, is the second. You are the third.'

'What about the police?'

'They have a number of unsolved incidents they're dealing with. I believe a large percentage, if not all of them, are related to the theory I'm working on.'

'Haven't you involved them yet?'

Miles shook his head. 'And I won't until I'm absolutely convinced there's something to be concerned about. If news of a possible threat from mutated scorpions leaked out there would be a mass exodus from this area. Panic. Chaos. Unfortunately we're in the middle of the holiday period. Thousands of people. And cars. If they all tried to leave at once . . . well . . . '

'I see what you mean.' Jill fell silent for a moment. 'But you can't guarantee it won't happen, either. It's obvious that there's been no actual sighting of these creatures. If there had the news would be spread by now. Everyone would be talking about it.'

'There is one thing I haven't told you yet,' Miles said. 'Possibly you won't thank me when I do tell you.'

'Now that sounds positively ominous.'

'Certain important facts were not revealed to the public at the time of the Long Point outbreak — or after. When the original nest was discovered, though the scorpions had already abandoned it, they had left behind one or two specimens too sick to travel. They were in fact dying. It was realised that these scorpions were different from the ones already on the loose. Most probably they were from a later breeding cycle, one in which the already mutated state had been taken a step further on.'

'In what way?'

'Their size. They were in the region of two to three feet long.'

Jill stared out through the side window. 'And is this what you're worried about? That any scorpions here will be large ones?'

'Yes. Probably even larger than the ones in the Long Point nest. Over a year has passed, remember. Long enough for fresh breeding cycles, for the new strain to throw off its weak members and develop fully.'

'To what size? I mean are we going to get scorpions as big as horses?'

'No. There's a limit to how large they can grow. It's to do with the structure of their bodies. If they kept getting larger and larger they would eventually reach a point where their legs wouldn't be capable of supporting their bodies. I'd say we could expect scorpions of around three to four feet in length.'

Jill stared at him, disbelief clouding her face until she realised he meant every word he'd spoken. 'My God, you're serious, aren't you?'

'I'm afraid I am.'

'What can you do about it?'

'Try and destroy them before they attempt any kind of full-scale excursion.'

'And how will you do that?' She hesitated. 'You intend going down into those tunnels!'

'It's the only way to find out if these theories are correct. If they are then we have to destroy them at source. Where their nest is.' Miles smiled thinly. 'Believe me when I say the idea has little appeal. But it has to be done. And quickly.' He glanced at his watch. 'Fancy a drive across to Penzance? There are a few things I need to pick up before I set foot in those damn tunnels.'

Jill nodded. 'Yes, I'd like that very much.'

10

'Move along now, ladies and gentlemen! The performance is about to commence! Have your tickets ready and make sure you still have the kiddies with you, because we forgot to feed the lions today!'

The circus and its attendant sideshows spread out across the flat expanse of trampled grass known as Pendall Green. It was a wide, oval meadow bordering High Moor, just over three-quarters of a mile outside the town. It served as a base for the annual Farmers' Show in early summer and for the communal firework display and bonfire each November 5th. Between those dates Pendall Green was host to numerous displays, shows, events. Each year at this time the circus arrived and stayed for a week before moving on along the coast. The circus had played on Pendall Green every year for as long as anyone could recall and had become a popular event with the tourists.

The warm evening air throbbed to the sound of diesel generators mingling with the music that blared from loudspeakers high over the heads of the swelling crowds. The circus lured people like bees to a pot of honey. The gaudy colours and the tinny music. The transient nature of the performers; here today and gone tomorrow; their lives free for the most part from everyday restraints. It was one of the curiosities of human nature that no one ever considered the minus side. An uncertainty overshadowing the future of a dying way of life. Audiences were becoming smaller with each passing year. The old traditions were slipping away. Gone were the days when father passed on skills to the sons; as the old artistes faded away there were not always youngsters ready to step into the vacated spotlight. Financial burdens weighed heavily too. The cost of transporting a circus from site to site had become restrictive and it only took a couple of low attendances to practically wipe out the profit for a week.

Yet the spirit still remained and in the

old tradition the show went on, even if the smiles had become a little strained and the routines slightly jaded . . .

Vin Becker took a final drag on his cigarette, dropped it on the ground and crushed it out. He glanced at his watch. Time to get the lions ready! He strolled along the line of trailers, each containing a built-on cage, and stopped beside one. Vin glanced through the bars. There were four lions in the big cage. Three of them appeared placid — the fourth, the oldest beast in the group, was pacing back and forth, head down, tail swishing. A deep, disturbed growl issuing from its throat.

'Hey, Cassius, what's up with you?' Vin asked. He knew the lions as well as any human could know these independent beasts, and normally they were no trouble. Even this close to a performance they failed to get upset.

'What's the matter with him, Vin?' asked Sammy Crane, one of Vin's helpers.

'I don't know. Not like Cassius to get noisy 'fore he goes on. He's a lazy bugger.'

'Something's upset him, I reckon,'

Sammy insisted, pointing at the lion. 'He looks proper nasty. Stick your arm through those bars I reckon he'd have it off tonight.'

'Keep your eyes on him then,' Vin suggested.

Sammy waved his arm at a waiting group of men. With Vin guiding them the men began to roll the cage towards the big-top and the safety tunnel along which the lions would enter the main cage standing in the ring.

As they moved towards the big-top the other lions began to stir, adding their rumbling snarls to those coming from Cassius.

'Bloody hell!' one of the men exclaimed. 'I'm glad I ain't goin' in a cage with that bunch tonight . . . '

* * *

'I thought you brought me here to see the circus?' Sally Prentise said defensively.

'Yeah, well I reckon we'll make up our own act,' Bob Sharp grinned. He pulled the girl closer to him, confidently sliding his hand under her thin T-shirt, fingers seeking the taut curve of her breast.

'You can cut that out . . . ' Sally began coldly. Then she felt his fingers pressing into the soft flesh of her breast, squeezing and fondling, reaching the half-risen button of her nipple, and a delicious warmth flowed through her. It was like a teasing, liquid tingle, squirming its way down her body to the softly aching spot between her thighs. She moaned and let her body sag in surrender against Bob's. She turned her face to his, searching for his mouth with her moist lips.

'What . . . '

Bob jerked away and Sally stumbled off-balance. She threw out a hand to grab him.

'What is it?' she asked; half-angry, half-afraid at his sudden change of mood.

Bob was peering into the semi-darkness that lay around them. All he could see was a criss-cross patchwork of shadows thrown by the web of guy ropes and stretched canvas.

'I heard something,' he said.

'Could have been anything,' Sally

pointed out, her tone peeved now that she seemed on the point of being deprived of a promising episode. 'Somebody passing by. Animal. We *are* at a circus, you know.' She moved up behind him, slipping her arms round his waist. 'Bobbee,' she whispered, letting her hand move down the front of his tight jeans until she felt the soft bulge. 'Why don't we find somewhere quieter.' The softness beneath her fingers began to harden.

He twisted in her embrace until he was facing her. His arms circled her roughly. Without any kind of pretence at consideration he pulled her T-shirt up, exposing her breasts, and buried his face in the soft, scented flesh. Sally let her head fall back, mouth open in silent wonder, her eyes seeing the bright stars in the sky above her. She felt his hungry fingers tugging at her jeans, sliding them over her hips and down . . .

And then she heard the sound, too. They both turned. Curious. Wondering.

And saw . . .

* * *

Slowly the animals began to make their unrest felt. And within a short time the anxiety was transmitted from cage to cage, from the enclosure to the very circus ring itself. The beasts added their vocal discomfort, the rising cacophony breaking through the din of raised voices and music and pounding machinery.

Inside the main tent, despite the efforts of the performers, the audience became increasingly restless. Heads turned. Worried parents reassured their children, then glanced again at the exits.

'For God's sake go and 'ave a bleedin' look!'

Max Rosberg cleared his throat nervously and waved the hesitating figure away.

'Go on,' he snarled. 'I'll try and keep 'em quiet.'

Max tugged at his scarlet coat, adjusted his ringmaster's top hat, and strode confidently into the glare of the spotlights. He made an impatient gesture at the tall blonde woman standing in the centre of the ring. She glared at him, angry because he had walked on during her act. Max ignored her — which was difficult — because Olga Petrova was an extremely striking figure. He didn't like the way she was brandishing the three-foot Russian sabre, even though it was part of her act. Skirting her, Max made his way to the centre of the ring and raised the microphone he carried in his hand.

'Ladies and Gentlemen! Please do not allow the slight disturbance outside to interfere with your enjoyment of the show. I can assure you it is nothing more than a little restlessness amongst the animals and will be dealt with shortly. Now I will leave you in the capable hands of the beautiful Madame Olga.'

Max edged his way out of the ring, conscious of Olga's angry scowl. He hurried down the ramp and emerged outside the tent to a scene of utter confusion.

People — public and circus alike — were milling around in groups. Above the clamour of the circus and the sideshows could be heard the agitated sounds of the animals. Max stood and listened, puzzled and then alarmed, because he'd never heard anything like it in his life before. Yet it conveyed the state of the animals plainly. They were frightened. Even terrified.

Max began to walk towards the distant cages.

Something had scared the animals.

But what?

He heard the first scream then. High and shrill. A human voice. A sound filled with sheer terror.

Max hesitated, his steps faltering. He wasn't sure what he might find.

More screams. Coming from the other side of the circus area.

'What the bloody hell is going on?' Max demanded, but his words were lost in the general din.

From behind a parked trailer a figure lurched into view. Running. Stumbling. Arms thrashing the air wildly. Staring eyes shone out of a white face. Mouth open in a long, continuous scream.

Max ran forward, towards the figure.

The man fell to his knees. Body jerking, twisting. And there appeared to be something clinging to his back.

Something long and dark that wriggled and humped.

As Max neared the crouching figure he was able to see more clearly. Details. Sharp, crystal clear details that made his mind recoil.

There, now illuminated by the powerful floodlights, was the thing clinging to the screaming man's back. Its shell-like body reflecting the harsh light, bristled legs constantly moving as it maintained its balance. Curving, pincered arms splayed out over the unprotected back of its cowering victim. Even as Max watched, the thing plunged the cruel pincers down, severing flesh and muscle. There was a rush of thick blood from the hideous wound. The man gave a despairing cry and threw himself face down on the ground, his clawing fingers gouging furrows in the hard earth. The creature ignored his screams and his squirming. With cold and deliberate intent it lowered its head and tore at the raw flesh edging the wound.

Max turned away, his stomach heaving. The bright lights and the blaring music exploded around him. Over all other sounds he could hear the rising crescendo of screams and shouts. They were coming from all directions. He clamped his hands over his ears and lurched off toward his own trailer. Whatever was causing all the uproar could stay outside. All Max wanted to do was to get inside and lock the door. And stay there until everything was back to normal.

Someone ran out of the darkness and smashed headlong into Max. He felt himself flung to the ground. His head struck some hard object. He rolled, groaning, dizzy, the sick feeling in his stomach rising. He put a trembling hand to the back of his head and felt the warm stickiness of blood on his fingers. He tried to sit up. He was unable to control his actions and found himself on his back again, staring up into the night sky. He lay for a moment, hoping the giddiness would pass. Without warning the star filled sky was blotted out. For a moment he thought he'd gone blind. Then the darkness shifted and Max realised something was hanging over him, blocking out the sky. He couldn't make out what it was at first. Then his eyes adjusted and he was able to see the expressionless features, the loathsome eyes regarding him with total indifference. A moist slit opened to show jagged teeth in a mouth that oozed saliva. Max yelled and threw up a hand to ward off the apparition. He felt something strike his arm. There was no pain at first. Just a rush of warm blood that spilled onto his upturned face. Then Max caught a glimpse of his hand, blood pulsing thickly from the severed stumps of his fingers. A solid weight pressed against his chest. He felt scrabbling legs gripping his body. A sudden stale stench filled his nostrils. Max heaved, felt vomit rush up his throat. He choked it back. A rigid hardness touched his lower jaw. Clamped it. Max felt the pressure increase. Bone grated. Moved. Flesh tore. Blood surged into his mouth. He tried to dislodge the object gripping his jaw. His attempts went unnoticed. The brutal pressure increased. The bone on one side of his jaw splintered. There was a savage pulling motion and Max's lower jaw, in its entirety, was ripped out. Blood and shredded flesh spilled from the huge wound, more of it flooding Max's throat, quickly beginning to choke him.

* * *

The scorpions had circled the circus area, advancing slowly until they were sure of themselves. Then they moved in quickly, attracted by the scents and sounds. The bright lights lured them too, though they were unsure why. They scuttled through the darkness of the perimeter in their dozens, waiting briefly in the gloom before venturing further.

And then, as though prompted by some unheard, unseen command they scuttled forward, moving through the outlying shadows to erupt in a nightmarish flood. A young couple preparing for an excursion into adolescent sexual enlightenment were the first victims. Their awareness of the scorpions' presence dawned late and they died swiftly, though in terrible agony, their pale bodies torn apart in a fevered frenzy.

The main body of the scorpions descended on the unsuspecting crowds thronging the circus area, turning enjoyment into fear, laughter into cries of pain and horror . . .

* * *

Vin Becker reached the door of his trailer, flung it open and lunged inside. In the darkness he collided with a piece of furniture, banging his knee against some hard projection. Swearing loudly he groped for the light switch. As light flooded the trailer Vin limped to a tall cupboard. He yanked open the door, reaching inside for the rifle propped in a corner. In all his years with the circus he'd never had to use the weapon; not that it mattered. It had always been a comfort to know it was there in the event of something happening with one of the animals. Now, as he lifted it, the thought of having to use it unsettled him.

Vin quickly loaded, dropping spare cartridges into his pocket. In his mind he was forming a picture of the things he'd seen and what they had been doing. Even now he desperately hoped it was a weird nightmare, but the horror outside *was* real. He could hear the chaotic din through the walls; the shrieks and the screams; the frantic sounds of the frightened animals — and he knew that it was no dream.

He pushed open the door and ran, heading towards the animal cages. He was fond of his charges. Took a pride in caring for them. The thought of them coming to harm enraged him.

Reaching the cage area he saw one of the scorpions tearing at the bars of the tiger's cage. Already the metal bars were bending under the onslaught. The large Bengal tiger had backed into a corner where it crouched and watched the intruder. Vin put the rifle to his shoulder, aimed and fired. The bullet struck the scorpion midway along its squirming body, blasting a pulpy exit hole as it emerged. The force ripped the scorpion away from the cage, tossing it along the ground. The creature writhed violently, its arched tail whipping back and forth.

Working a fresh round into the breech Vin moved closer. He failed to repress a shudder as he gazed down. It sensed his closeness and made a frantic attempt to reach him. Vin took a hasty step back and calmly fired again. The bullet tore through the ugly head, just above the gleaming eyes. The scorpion arched almost double before it became still.

A harsh sound behind caused Vin to turn. He saw a human figure, on hands and knees, a scorpion clinging to his back. Vin ran up close and fired into the scorpion's body, knocking it to the ground.

'Here, mate, give me your hand . . . ' Vin said.

The victim raised his head. Glistening strips of shredded flesh hung from his lacerated cheeks. The left eye had been clawed from the socket, leaving behind a bloody hole.

Vin was debating what to do when he heard a brittle rattle of sound. He turned, swinging the rifle round with him, sensing, rather than actually seeing the scorpion's slashing pincer. There was a hard jolt against his left arm. The impact was strong enough to numb his arm and it blanked off the initial pain. But Vin *saw* the tattered flesh of his arm. The white bone gleaming through the blood. He took an uncertain step back, trying to line up the rifle for a swift shot. It never came. His attempt to ward off the inevitable was feeble and bound to fail.

The scorpion lunged forward and up, pincers extended. They met momentary resistance. And then weak human flesh gave way. The claws savaged and rent the flesh, penetrating muscle with ease, splintering bone, drawing forth a vivid flood of rich, warm blood.

* * *

The majority of scorpions moved swiftly back and forth across the trampled ground, seeking their prey with ease. But here and there one moved with an uncertainty of co-ordination, slithering to the ground, legs moving weakly as it tried to stand again. In a shadowed corner, beside some parked trailers, one of these creatures stood, head sagging. It jerked with a violent spasm, and dark fluid dribbled from its open mouth. The body was crusted with open sores that oozed a stinking pus.

In the horror of the moment these events passed unnoticed, their significance lost to those gripped in the struggle to survive.

* * *

The audience made a mass rush for the main tent's exits. Those who were fortunate to break free found that they were no better off. More scorpions scuttled menacingly about the circus area. The people emerging from the large tent caught their attention and groups of the squirming dark mutations began to move towards them.

Already the ground was littered with the dead and the injured. Some scorpions ignored the people coming out of the tent and carried on with their terrible meal, seemingly satisfied with the victims they already had.

A group were at large inside the big tent.

They scuttled across the trampled grass and sawdust and began to attack the rear of the crowd desperately trying to force their way out. Screaming men, women and children were dragged to the ground. Their kicking, squirming bodies mutilated and savaged by the frenzied creatures.

Olga Petrova, alone in the centre of the ring, found herself menaced by a single scorpion. It crawled over the wooden blocks edging the ring and advanced towards her. Olga stood her ground. The creature fascinated her. She knew it was a threat to her. That made little difference. Olga enjoyed a challenge. She smiled to herself as the repulsive thing edged closer. It appeared to be studying her closely. It was probably having difficulty understanding why she wasn't screaming or running like all the others.

Without warning it rose on its bristled legs, throwing out the clawed arms and arching its tail over its back.

Olga held herself motionless a few

seconds longer. Then, in the instant the scorpion moved in her direction, she brought up her right hand, in which she held the glittering sabre. The curved blade flashed against the bright spotlights. It became a blur as Olga made three powerful passes. The first removed the deadly sting from the tip of the tail. Each of the remaining strokes severed a claw from the end of the flexing arms. The scorpion fell back. Olga, a smile on her face, advanced, the deadly blade swishing back and forth, cutting, slashing, severing, until the scorpion lay twitching and dying in the sawdust ring.

Olga hurried to the side-wall of the huge tent. With a swift stroke of the sabre's edge she opened a slit in the canvas and stepped outside.

It was as if she had planted herself in the middle of a madhouse. Bedlam reigned supreme. The air was filled with the screams of the hurt and the frightened, both animal and human. Figures ran back and forth, some pursued by the scuttling black creatures that had crawled out of the night. Others writhed on the ground, already victim to claw and sting. Circus animals, freed from their enclosures, ran riot, causing as much damage as the ravaging scorpions.

A howling chimpanzee leaped and rolled around in a frenzy as it tried to dislodge the scorpion clinging to its furry back. One of the beautiful Arab stallions, its eyes rolling in terror, galloped past Olga. Three scorpions clung to its bloody sides, driving their stings into the quivering flesh. The stallion ran on for another twenty yards before its legs collapsed and it pitched to the ground.

Olga shook her head in disbelief at the carnage. She had never seen anything like this before. She ran across the trampled grass, realising that she had to get clear of the area if she was to survive. There was no way of fighting these creatures. There were too many of them. And the people were in a panic. Too much of a panic to do any good for themselves.

A shrill sound made Olga turn her head. Her eyes widened in alarm. One of the full-grown Indian elephants, dragging its tether chain, was thundering through the crowds, scattering people in all directions. The dark shapes of a number of scorpions could be seen clinging to its leathery hide. The elephant was in full flight, trumpeting shrilly in terror. Olga threw up her arms as the beast loomed before her, her voice raised in a wild shout. There was no stopping the elephant. Olga was trampled underfoot, her body left crushed and bloody in the dirt.

The stampeding elephant abruptly changed direction. It smashed heavily against one of the mobile hot-dog trailers, the flimsy construction splintering as it hit the ground. The containers of hot oil spilled, badly burning the operator. Even while he was attempting to claw his way out of the wreckage the oil was ignited by the still-burning gas jet. There was a vivid flash as the trailer engulfed in flame. Burning oil showered across the area, setting clothing alight. Some of the oil was sprayed onto nearby awnings. Within minutes the fire had spread along a line of stalls, reaching down to eat at the main structure and their contents.

The rising flames and the smoke added to the general confusion. Red-hot sparks burst from the blaze, raining down on the scattering crowds *and* the attacking scorpions.

It was only then, as the billowing flames reached out to claim scorpion victims, that the creatures broke off the attack. They began to retreat. Scuttling into the darkness, seeming to find security in the shadows.

They left behind a ravaged and desolated circus. Frightened, hysterical crowds. Dead and injured.

For the scorpions it was a beginning. Their first major foray. Though there was no way yet of knowing it was also the beginning of the end for them . . .

11

'You were right,' Jill said. 'The food *is* good here.'

Miles nodded as he forked a piece of steak from his plate. 'I've always found it pretty reliable.'

'May I have some more of that wine?'

As he filled her glass Miles glanced at his watch. 'I'd like to get back to Port Pendall as soon as we've finished here.'

'Fine with me.'

'I hate having to spoil the day but . . . '

A nervous smile crossed Jill's face. 'I must be the first girl to be stood up for a scorpion!'

Miles couldn't hold down his laughter. 'When this is all over I'll make it up to you.'

'You smooth-talking entomologists are all the same.'

They finished their meal in unhurried silence. Miles paid the bill and they walked out of the small, dark-brown restaurant into the late afternoon warmth. Around them surged the tourist-swollen population of Penzance. Miles guided Jill down a narrow alley and they emerged on the edge of the car park where he had left the Range Rover. Miles eased the big vehicle out of the park, drove steadily through Penzance and onto the A30. Once clear of the town Miles pushed the accelerator down and the powerful engine thrust the Range Rover along the road.

'When do you intend going down the mine?' Jill asked, broaching the subject they had both been able to erase from their minds during the last couple of hours.

Miles sighed. 'I'd meant doing it today. That's why I tried to hurry the meal along.' He glanced at Jill. 'I apologise for that.'

'No need,' she said. 'Miles, I've enjoyed today.'

'It wasn't all that special. The way I made you stand around in that gun shop.'

'If the company's right the place doesn't matter. And today the company *was* right.' Jill was silent for a moment.

'You will be careful — going into that place I mean?'

'As careful as I can be. I don't intend to take any chances. All I want to do is establish one way or another that there *are* scorpions in that mine. Right now I don't intend doing anything about them. Not until I have help.'

'How will you get that?'

'By informing the police. And then devising the swiftest and surest way of destroying the scorpions and any nests before they can cause too much trouble.'

Leaving the A30 Miles cruised along winding, green fringed lanes that carried him directly to Port Pendall. It was almost eight o'clock when they reached the town.

'You're not going to the mine tonight, Miles?'

He shook his head. 'No. I need a good night's rest.' He grinned. 'I've just realised I haven't been to bed for almost twenty-four hours. Wouldn't do to go stumbling around half asleep.'

He brought the Range Rover to a halt on the street running along the harbour front. The lowering sun cast rich red shadows on the gentle swell of water in the bay. The evening sky was streaked like burnished copper and high overhead gulls wheeled and spun, their shrill cries ringing out over the harbour.

'It's beautiful,' Jill said.

'Yes,' Miles agreed. 'Doesn't matter how many times I visit Cornwall — I'm always finding new delights.'

'Do you come often?'

'Not as often as I'd like.' He gazed at her lovely profile. 'What about you?'

'I fell in love with the place my first visit years ago. I just keep coming back.'

Miles put the Range Rover in gear. 'Well, this won't find me a bed for the night.'

'Lord, haven't you booked a room?'

'No. I drove straight to the mine when I'd finished my business in town.'

'But you'll never get a room in Port Pendall. Not at this time of year. It's the height of the season.'

'I hadn't even thought about that.'

Jill sighed. 'Men! You can land a spaceship on the moon but you can't even look after yourselves properly.'

'That's what appeals to you women. Our helplessness. Brings out your mothering instinct.'

'Well my instinct is telling me to offer you a roof over your head for the night.'

'Oh?'

'Look, I've got a large cottage with four bedrooms — three of which are empty. Please, Miles, be my guest.'

'All right,' Miles said. 'And thanks.'

It took them twenty minutes to reach the cottage. In the fading light Miles caught a glimpse of a rambling, thatched-roof building. It was surrounded by green lawns and lush hedges. Jill climbed out to open the double gates giving access to a gravel drive. Easing the Range Rover up behind Jill's parked car — a gleaming Jaguar XJ6 — Miles switched off the engine. He climbed out and walked round to the rear of the vehicle. Lifting the tailgate door he took out a number of wrapped packages. By the time he'd locked up Jill was inside. He followed her in, depositing his packages on the floor of the lounge.

'I'll make some coffee,' Jill said over her shoulder as she moved to the kitchen.

'Mind if I make a call?' Miles asked, indicating the telephone.

'Go ahead. Phone book's under the coffee table.'

'Thanks. I know the number.'

Miles dialled the Port Pendall Hospital, asking the switchboard for Richard Groves's office. Groves's phone rang only twice before it was picked up.

'Miles?' Groves's voice was urgent. 'Thank God you called. I didn't know how to contact you.'

'Sorry, I should have kept in touch,' Miles apologised. 'What's wrong?'

'They're on the loose, Miles. You were right! The scorpions have made a mass attack on a circus outside town. The reports started coming in a half-hour ago.'

'Where is this circus?'

'Pendall Green. Can you get there?'

'Yes. I'll meet you there. And, Richard, get your police inspector there, too!' Putting down the phone Miles went to the kitchen door. 'Jill, forget the coffee, love, and tell me if you know where Pendall Green is.'

Jill came out of the kitchen. She watched Miles unwrap one of the packages he'd brought from Penzance. 'Yes, I know where it is. Why?'

'Because I've got to get there quickly.' Miles removed the final wrapping and exposed the polished wood and blued metal of a pump-action shotgun. From a smaller package he extracted a box of cartridges. He loaded the gun, checking that it was ready for use.

'Does that mean . . . ?' Jill began.

'I'm afraid it does,' Miles said. 'The scorpions have shown themselves — in force.'

'I'll show you where the Green is.'

* * *

It took just under a quarter-of-an-hour to reach Pendall Green. They were able to see the place long before they arrived. The night sky glowed with a dull orange light. Thick clouds of smoke hung over the area.

'It looks awful,' Jill commented as they neared the Green.

Miles was watching the line of vehicles still driving away. He caught the odd glimpse of scared faces and crying children being soothed by harassed parents. He spotted a couple of ambulances too, sirens insisting that the traffic allow them to pass, blue lamps flashing with cold light.

'You turn in just ahead,' Jill said. 'There!'

'I see it.'

Miles drove off the road and down the gentle slope that brought them onto Pendall Green. The circus lay before them, a scene of devastation and chaos. The entire area appeared to be ringed by police cars, fire appliances and ambulances, all with flashing lights. A cacophony of sound swelled from the scene; the metallic clatter of engines and generators, the rushing sound of the rising flames, and the lesser sound of frightened animals *and* people.

'Here comes the law,' Jill said.

Miles wound down his window as a

burly, wide-shouldered police sergeant made his way toward him.

'And what are you doing exactly?' asked the sergeant.

'Looking for Dr Richard Groves, Sergeant,' Miles said. 'He's expecting me. My name's Miles Ranleigh.'

'Oh, I see. All right, sir, drive straight on down to that dark blue Triumph. The doctor's there with Inspector Braddock.'

Miles nodded and coasted down the slope. As Miles parked beside the Triumph, Richard Groves appeared and hurried round to Miles's door.

'Am I glad you're here,' he said as Miles climbed out.

'Hey, it's only Miles Ranleigh, not Superman.' Miles laughed. 'I don't expect to come up with any bright ideas just yet.'

Sam Braddock, who had been standing back a little, listening quietly, moved forward. 'Mr Ranleigh, all *I* want is help — in any form.'

'Miles, this is Inspector Sam Braddock.'

Braddock gave an all-embracing wave of his hand, taking in the entire circus area. 'This is all a little hard to accept in one breath.'

'I realise that, Inspector, and without wanting to appear offhand all I can suggest is that you take that breath so we can start to get organised.'

'You're talking like a man who's anticipating something,' Braddock said. 'What is it?'

'If the scorpions are able to mount a concentrated attack like tonight's, I'd hazard a guess that their numbers must be pretty high. They've obviously reached a stable point in their mutated development. If my guess is correct we could be in for a lot more attacks.'

'Along the lines of this one?'

'Yes.'

'With the area jammed solid with tourists those damn things could enjoy a massacre a day.' Braddock shook his head in frustration. 'So what do we do? Evacuate the Pendall Bay area?'

'I have a feeling an evacuation will be under way shortly,' Miles said. 'A lot of the people who were here tonight are going to leave the moment they pack their bags. And they'll pass on the story to others.'

'Jesus wept!' Braddock muttered. 'This is going to sound great when I phone it through to Division. They'll never believe me.'

'Send them a few pictures of what's happened here,' Miles suggested. 'They'll believe you.'

'Do you want to have a look round yourself?' Groves asked.

'The idea doesn't exactly thrill me but I'd better.'

Miles turned and walked to the Range Rover. 'Jill, I'm going to take a look at what's happened. Wait here for me.'

'All right. Miles, be careful.'

He nodded and rejoined the others. They walked down towards the main circus area.

'Apparently the evening performance was well under way when the attack took place. There was so much going on that no one noticed the scorpions until it was too late.' Sam Braddock paused to have a quick word with a uniformed policeman before rejoining Miles and Richard

Groves. 'By the time people realised something was wrong the place had been overrun. From what we've got in the way of preliminary statements it would appear that it was a deliberate attack. Is that possible, Mr Ranleigh?'

'We found during the Long Point incident that these mutant scorpions have the ability to band together for the good of the group. That's normally something a scorpion wouldn't do. But we have to remember that we're dealing with a new species here. It's entirely possible that their mental capabilities have altered along with their physical make-up.'

'Miles — over here,' Groves said. He led the way to where a dark shape lay at the base of an overturned ice cream kiosk. 'One of the circus people pointed this one out to me,' he explained. 'He shot it himself — but he said it was acting strangely. As if it were drunk, he said. It couldn't walk in a straight line. Kept falling down.'

'*Did it*?' Miles murmured. He stared at the dead scorpion. The first thing he noticed was the awful stench rising from it. And then the deep, open sores marking its body.

He crouched down to look more closely. All his preconceived ideas — even his preparedness — vanished as he found himself confronted by an actual scorpion. His gaze moved over it, from the cruel pincers, stained with dried blood, along the hard body to the curved tail with its menacing sting protruding from the bulbous poison-sac.

'It might be dead but it still frightens me,' Braddock murmured.

Miles didn't reply. Eventually he straightened up.

'Richard, I'd like to get this scorpion back to your department as soon as possible.'

'I'll arrange it.'

'See to it that whoever moves it is well protected. On no account let anyone touch it with bare hands. Stress that point, Richard. And you'd better have your department sealed off.'

Groves nodded and turned away.

'Do I detect an added complication?' Braddock asked.

Miles gave a quick smile. 'You noticed. I've a suspicion this scorpion was dying long before it came here tonight. I think it was dead before that bullet hit it.'

'What was it dying of?'

'At the moment I'm not certain. But I'll hazard a guess that it has something to do with the mutation process. I should know more after I've carried out a dissection.'

'Are you talking about some kind of infectious disease? Is that why you don't want anyone touching the thing?'

Miles nodded. 'Keep it to yourself for the moment, Inspector. Let's be sure of our facts first. In the meantime it won't hurt to pass out a warning to your people about handling any of the dead scorpions. Any that are found should be soaked with petrol and burned where they are. And let's get everyone away from the area except those on official business.'

'Whatever you say, Mr Ranleigh.'

Miles stared at the dead scorpion. *Damn you! As if we haven't got enough problems! Now this!*

'Inspector, it might be a good idea to

form some teams of men to check the area,' Miles suggested. 'See if they can spot any scorpions still in the vicinity.'

'I'd better see what I can do about arming them.' Braddock scratched his cheek. 'Tell me, Mr Ranleigh, just how do you kill a bloody four-foot scorpion?'

'Without any practical experience I decided on a shotgun.' Picked one up in Penzance earlier. The spread-pattern would be useful against a number of targets and a shot to the head should be enough to stop even one of these things!'

'Let's hope you're right,' Braddock said. 'Let's hope we're *both* right. We won't be getting many second chances if we're not!'

GENERATION

12

Trevor Parkinson drove slowly up the dusty, rutted track leading to the Needham farm. More than once during the journey from town he'd had to resist the urge to turn round and drive back to Port Pendall. He wasn't looking forward to what he had to do and he knew it wouldn't be easy or pleasant. But it had to be done.

He caught sight of the farmhouse and outbuildings, black against the night sky. He wished now that he'd made his visit during daylight, but pressure of work had meant cancelling his daytime free periods for the past week. Somehow, coming during the hours of darkness seemed to add to the already solemn mood he was in.

Since that first contact between Linda and himself Parkinson had known that a confrontation was on the cards. Each time he'd been with her since then had only strengthened their feelings for each other. Without resorting to self-pity Linda had made him realise that her relationship with Jim was over. Parkinson's regret for his friend was shortlived. He wanted Linda more than he'd ever wanted a woman before. The fact that he was going to hurt Jim didn't deter him. Even so he wasn't looking forward to the meeting tonight . . .

The rear wheels of Parkinson's car locked as he stamped on the brake. He leaned forward to stare through the dusty windscreen. He could see the low-lying shape of the old house, a light showing in one of the downstairs windows. Light streamed from an open doorway, laying a pool of yellow across the yard. At first glance the scene appeared normal — yet there was something indefinable in the air that unsettled him. He sat watching the house for a time. It was too quiet. Suddenly he grinned. He was playing policeman too damn hard and tonight he was supposed to be off duty.

He drove the rest of the way to the house, turning the car so that it was facing back down the track. He climbed out, then paused again to stare at the building. There was no getting away from the fact that it *was* unusually quiet and the wide open front door only added to his unease.

He hesitated on the low step at the door.

'Anyone home?' he called for want of a better way of announcing his presence.

There was no reply.

Then he heard a faint, dry scuttering from deep inside the house. The noise was brief, leaving hollow silence in its wake.

Parkinson began to think he'd have been better off somewhere else. He should have talked Linda into doing this differently. He sighed. *Sod it!* Better get it over with.

He stepped inside.

It was warm and cloying in the stone-flagged hallway, the air heavy, clinging to him like soft wool. A musky odour reminiscent of bad meat filled his nostrils. Wrinkling his nose in disgust he moved along the hall toward the kitchen.

The smell intensified and his stomach began to churn. He heard again the soft scuttling. Other sounds began to reach him, too: moist sucking and tearing.

Taking a single step forward he pushed open the kitchen door. The wide, low-ceilinged room, looked like a slaughterhouse. Blood was everywhere; pooled on the floor, splashed across walls and furniture. And at the centre of this nightmare two ravaged and mutilated bodies sprawled on the kitchen floor.

Parkinson was unable to tear his gaze from the sickening tableau before him. He had seen death before but no amount of previous experience could have guaranteed immunity against the stark horror confronting him now. Clustering around the lifeless bodies, their terrible pincers dripping with blood, five scorpions savagely mutilated the already shredded flesh of Jim and Linda Needham.

In the scant seconds it took to absorb the scene, Trevor Parkinson realised that Linda's once beautiful young body had been ripped open from breast to groin. He couldn't hold back a stunned groan at the sight of her tender flesh cruelly laid open to expose the glistening mass of internal organs . . . He threw up.

Disturbed by the noise one of the scorpions raised its gory head. Pitiless eyes regarded him coldly. The curved arms probed the air, pincers flexing. The open gash of mouth drooled bloody strings of sinew.

Held by those hypnotic eyes Parkinson stared helplessly. It was only as the scorpion broke away from its companions and scuttled towards him that he snapped out of his trancelike state. He jerked back from the doorway. Felt something grip the sleeve of his coat. In desperation he yanked his arm away. The sleeve ripped and Parkinson stumbled back, slamming against the wall. He caught his breath, struggled to retain his balance. Out of the corner of his eye he saw the rest of the dark, wriggling body emerging from the kitchen doorway. He turned, emitting a cry of pure terror, and hurled himself along the hallway, lunging for the outside door.

His foot caught the edge of the step

and he felt himself falling forward. He threw out both hands in an attempt to protect himself, succeeding only in tearing his palms on the rough ground. He twisted his body as he landed, ignoring the pain, his mind fully aware of the creature close behind. There was a momentary silence when he was able to hear the dry scrape of its approach. A sob of agony burst from his dry lips as he pushed up off the ground, throwing a quick glance over his shoulder.

The scorpion was in the doorway, pincers already thrust forward. The powerful claws still dappled with globules of blood. It arched its dark body, curving the flexible tail over its back.

Parkinson scrambled away as the thing burst through into the yard. A slashing pincer snagged his trousers, ripping a long gash in the material and grazing his leg. Parkinson arched his body to one side. He felt his right foot twist beneath him, his weight bearing down on the ankle. Something gave and white-hot pain exploded. He fell, sliding helplessly along the outside wall of the farmhouse.

The scorpion turned towards him, the raised tail starting to ease forward.

Sprawled against the base of the wall, Parkinson knew he wouldn't have a second chance. Instinctively, he started to edge away. His left hand nudged something leaning against the wall and fingers identified a smooth wooden handle. He gripped it automatically, seeking reassurance from the solid feel. His head turned, eyes focusing on the object in his hand. In the dim light from the open door he recognised the familiar shape of a double-edged axe.

Sound reached his ears — the scorpion raising itself on stiffened legs in preparation for its attack — and Parkinson realised he was close to death.

Without further thought he twisted his body round, reaching for the axe with his other hand. Grasping it he let himself roll onto his back, sensing the looming bulk above him. Sweat beaded his face as he inhaled the nauseating stench. Fighting the awkward position he was in, Parkinson dragged the axe up over his shoulders, driving it at the scorpion's lowering head. The blade bit into the shell-like outer skin, splitting it open. Dark fluid bubbled from the wound. The scorpion arched in a reflex action, pincers snapping viciously shut.

Parkinson placed a foot against the wall and thrust himself away from the house. He got his good foot under him and climbed to his feet, using the axe as support.

The stricken scorpion lunged wildly in his direction, striking blindly with its dripping sting. Parkinson found he could avoid it easily now. The deep laceration in its head appeared to have interfered with its sense of direction.

The scene in the farm kitchen came back to him. He thought of what the scorpions had been doing to Linda's body and he knew it would be a long time before he would be able to erase that sight from his mind.

A desperate, uncontrolled yell rose in his throat. Parkinson raised the axe, stepped in close, and drove the blade deep. As the glistening dark shell burst open, spewing out a mass of slimy pulp, the scorpion twisted violently, lashing out with snapping pincers. One closed around Parkinson's left calf, gripping tightly. He fought to free himself as he was drawn closer to the squirming creature, catching a glimpse of its gleaming eyes as the ugly head swung round to him. The raw gash of its mouth gaped open, dripping greasy mucus, and Parkinson shuddered with revulsion. He still had a grip on the axe and now he dragged it from the gaping wound. The creature lashed out with its sting. Trevor let his body fall back, lifting the axe, and the curved sting glanced off the steel blade. Before the scorpion could strike again Parkinson began to hack it to pieces.

He stopped suddenly, realising that the thing no longer moved. Staring down, Parkinson felt vomit rise in his throat and he stumbled away, hardly aware of the pain in his leg where the pincer had ripped the flesh.

It was then that he remembered the other scorpions. They might choose to leave the house at any time. He threw the axe aside and hobbled to his waiting car.

Wrenching open the door he threw himself into the driving seat. The engine caught the moment he turned the key. He put it in gear, spinning the rear wheels as he moved off with the throttle flat against the floor. It was only as he fought the sliding vehicle over the rough track that he eased off, slowing to a safer pace. He breathed a sigh of relief as the track ended and he rolled the car onto the hard road.

Driving in the direction of Port Pendall he became aware of the sticky substance on his hands. A fetid odour surrounded him. He slowed the vehicle to the side of the road and flicked on the interior light.

His hands, jacket and trousers, were slick with the yellow pus that had burst from the scorpion's punctured body. The putrid stench rising from it was overpowering. Parkinson stared at his outstretched hands. The palms were beginning to itch, seeming to crawl, as if infested by minute, invisible insects. He became aware too, of nausea building up in his stomach. He leaned back in his seat, a claustrophobic urgency sweeping over him. The interior of the car began to shrink, to close in on him. He felt stifled. Parkinson fumbled for the door handle. After a few frantic seconds he located it and rolled awkwardly out onto the road. He lay on the rough tarmac for a time and then clambered slowly to his feet, staring about with vision that was becoming swiftly blurred.

He began to limp away from the car, stumbling on heavy unco-ordinated feet. The sickness had flooded his entire body now. There was little deliberation in his movements. No definite direction in his line of travel. He simply staggered along the shadowed road. He fell often. Heavily. Yet seemed to ignore the pain.

He had travelled almost three hundred yards when his strength finally drained away. He slipped to his knees, head resting on his chest. A final spasm coursed through his body. Parkinson toppled face down on the road. He lay very still.

13

'Well?'

Miles didn't answer Braddock's question immediately. He crossed Richard Groves's office and helped himself to a mug of coffee from the Thermos jug. He took a long swallow, allowing himself a moment to wind down. He saw Jill watching him from the other side of the office and gave her a quick smile.

'That scorpion in there is riddled with a bacillus which is causing a gangrenous condition, possibly highly contagious.'

'*Gangrene!*' Braddock jerked up out of his seat. 'Are you sure?'

Miles nodded. 'It looks as if those scorpions are dying on their feet. Simply rotting away inside.'

'Any ideas why?'

'Perhaps some imbalance in the gene-structure of this new generation.' Miles shrugged. 'It could be an after effect of the radiation from Long Point.'

'Can it be passed to humans?'

'I'd say yes.' Miles sat down, deep in thought. 'Inspector, we have two priorities,' he said. 'First we have to locate and destroy the scorpions' nest. Everything *must* be wiped out to make sure no infection is left behind.'

'Secondly?'

'Place severe restrictions on movement in any area we designate. If the infection starts to spread it could cause more problems than the scorpions themselves.'

'How do you intend tackling the nest when you find it?' Braddock asked.

'We'll need a small team of men to go down into that mine with me.'

'You tell me how many and I'll provide them.'

'They'll need to be armed,' Miles said. 'And we'll need a damn good back-up on the surface. We might have to come out of there in a bloody hurry.'

'You'll have your back-up,' Braddock promised. 'Anything else?'

'Something I just thought of. We need an effective way of dealing with the nesting area. A way of destroying any young scorpions, eggs, and also possible sources of the infection. I can't think of anything more potent than fire. Could you see what you can do about getting your hands on a couple of flame-throwers. I expect the military would be the best people for that kind of hardware.'

'I'll make a few phone calls,' Braddock said. 'I'm not going to be very popular waking people at this time of night, but what the hell.'

'I think we should all try and snatch a few hours sleep before morning,' Miles suggested.

'Fine with me,' Braddock said. 'We'll meet near the mine between eight-thirty and nine.'

Miles scribbled Jill's telephone number on a pad sheet and handed it to Braddock. 'If you need me for *anything* before morning I'll be at this number.'

Left alone with Jill, Miles relaxed. He was tired now. His eyes felt heavy, gritty, and he found it difficult to keep them open. He drank the rest of his coffee and placed the empty mug on the desk.

'Shall we go?' he said.

Jill followed him out of the hospital building. The night air was slightly cooler now. Miles took deep breaths as they walked across to the parked Range Rover. He stood beside the vehicle and took out his keys, fumbling awkwardly as he tried to unlock the driver's door. He muttered to himself when the key jammed in the lock. A slim, warm hand was laid over his own, firmly easing his fingers away from the key.

'Here, let me do that,' Jill said. 'You're in no fit state to do any driving. Go on round to the other side and I'll let you in.'

Miles was too tired to argue. He climbed in and sank gratefully on the comfortable leather seat. He heard the powerful engine burst into life then settle to a muted roar. The sound lulled him and he closed his eyes. He experienced a gentle swaying motion as the vehicle moved off, then knew no more until Jill gently shook him awake.

'Come on, we're home,' she told him.

Miles clambered groggily out of the Range Rover and followed Jill inside.

'I'll fetch some clean sheets and make

up a bed for you,' she said.

Miles wandered across the lounge. He spotted a long couch, leaned the shotgun he was carrying against the side and sat down. It felt good. He slipped off his shoes and swung his long legs up onto the couch. Placing a cushion under his head he allowed himself to drift off into an exhausted sleep.

That was how Jill found him when she returned with an armful of blankets and sheets. She stood gazing down at him, then sighed and covered him with the blankets. Switching off all the lights except a small lamp she made her way up the stairs to her own room.

* * *

The aroma of freshly brewed coffee filled Miles's nostrils as he woke. Brilliant sunlight was streaming in through the windows and he lay for a while before pushing aside the blankets and sitting up. He located his shoes and put them on, allowing his nose to direct him towards the kitchen.

It was a large, sunny room fitted with modern units and equipment. Miles paused in the doorway to watch Jill as she dropped strips of bacon into a pan. Her thin cotton robe moulded itself to her supple figure as she moved across the kitchen.

'Morning,' he said.

She turned, smiling. She had that warm, slightly tousled look about her that suggested she hadn't been long out of bed herself.

'Hello. Did you sleep well?'

'I guess I did. Obviously I didn't make it any further than the couch.'

Jill poured him a large cup of strong coffee. 'You looked so comfortable I couldn't see any point in waking you.'

'Last night I could have slept on a clothesline.'

'Are you hungry? There's bacon, eggs, mushrooms.'

'Sounds great.'

'Sit down.'

'Has there been anything on the radio about last night?' Miles asked.

'Yes.' Jill reached across to turn on a

radio sitting on the worktop. 'Listen.'

A record was just ending. As the music faded, a station identity jingle was followed by a local news report.

There was a swift and precise bulletin about the events at the circus. Then the taut explanation that the authorities had decided to close off the Port Pendall area due to the unusually large influx of insect swarms. To prevent any undue distress or suffering it had been decided to keep the area as clear as possible until something could be done.

'They're playing it down,' Miles said. 'Not a word about scorpions.'

The news-reader went on to mention the traffic jams caused by the hundreds of vehicles trying to leave the area. Unfortunately, there had been a number of wild and exaggerated claims concerning the previous nights events and a lot of people had acted out of unjustified fears.

'He wouldn't be saying that if he'd had one of those things trying to tear his leg off!' Miles observed.

'I suppose they just want to keep some kind of order,' Jill said. 'Most people will accept the explanation and leave quietly.'

'Don't get me wrong,' Miles said. 'If I wasn't involved I'd be doing exactly the same thing.'

Jill placed his breakfast in front of him and sat down.

'Help yourself to more coffee,' she said.

'Thanks.' Miles topped up his cup. He switched off the radio. 'Let's forget about that mess for a while. Now tell me what *you* do when you're not on holiday in Cornwall.'

Jill stared at him for a moment. A smile edged the corners of her mouth. 'That came from nowhere didn't it?'

'It just occurred to me I know very little about you, and that I'd like to know more.'

'I was fortunate in having fairly wealthy parents. Being an only child I inherited everything when they both died in an air crash about eight years ago. It left me independent and able to pursue whatever kind of life I chose. I'd always been interested in fashion so I opened my own shop in London. We specialise in designing and making clothes exclusively for our own clients.'

'Do you design yourself?'

Jill nodded. 'Yes. I think I can say without appearing immodest that I'm pretty good at it.' She laughed softly. 'Does that sound terrible?'

'Not at all.'

'Miles — I can't help thinking about what you're going to do today. Going down that mine. Do you have to?'

'Yes. I'm involved. I couldn't back away from things now even if I wanted to. But don't worry. I'm not the heroic type. I value my life too highly to take unnecessary chances.'

'Please be careful,' Jill said. She stood up and came round to where Miles was sitting. Leaning towards him she put her arms around his neck and pressed her cheek against his. 'Do be careful,' she whispered. She kissed him quickly on the cheek then drew away and walked out of the kitchen.

Miles got up and followed her. She had crossed the lounge and was staring out through the French windows that opened onto the rear garden. He laid his hands on her slim shoulders.

Jill glanced back at him. 'I don't know why I did that,' she said.

'I'm just glad you did. I'd like to think it was because you care what happens to me. I have a feeling you're that kind of person. One who does care about others. These days knowing someone like that is a bonus.'

'Miles Ranleigh, you are a very nice person.'

He laughed. 'This is starting to sound like mutual admiration. I think we ought to stop it. And I know just how.'

'Oh?' Jill turned, raising her face to his. Under her smooth tan her flawless cheeks were gently flushed.

Miles kissed her gently, feeling her lips part under his own. Her arms drew tight around his neck and as his big hands pressed the soft curve of her body closer he felt the warmth of her flesh through the thin robe.

'I hope we know what we're doing,' she said quietly, studying him with sparkling eyes.

'I'm sure we do.'

‘What time are you meeting Inspector Braddock? Around nine wasn’t it?’

A gentle smile edged Miles’s mouth. ‘At least nine o’clock.’

‘That gives us plenty of time,’ Jill said. ‘Plenty of time!’

14

'I feel a bloody idiot in this thing!' Sam Braddock grumbled.

Miles glanced up from checking his shotgun. He couldn't help smiling at the sight of Braddock scowling at him through the open visor of the bulky protective suit he was wearing.

'It was the best protection we could get at such short notice,' he said.

Braddock leaned against the side of a parked police van. 'The sooner we get this done the better I'm going to feel.'

A similarly suited figure approached. Miles recognised the face of Sergeant Alex McCabe, the man in charge of the flame-thrower squad the army had sent along. As well as three flame-throwers the army had supplied the heavy protective suits.

'Ready when you are, Mr Ranleigh,' McCabe said. He was a tall, broad-shouldered man. Quiet yet plainly capable.

'Let's get it over with, shall we.'

The three of them walked across to where McCabe's three men waited alongside two of Braddock's.

'There aren't any rules for what we're doing today,' Miles said. 'We can't be sure what we'll find, but it's possible we'll see some unpleasant sights. As for the scorpions themselves — well we've all seen the photographs taken after last night's attack at the circus. We know the size of the things. Remember that they *are* dangerous. I don't want anyone taking chances. These scorpions can move pretty fast and those pincers are just as much a threat as the sting.' Miles hesitated. 'One more thing. This infection they carry. We all saw the results of that on Constable Parkinson. What happened to him can happen to any of us if we become infected. When we come out of the mine Dr Groves and his people will make sure we're not contaminated.' Miles glanced at Braddock. 'Anything you want to say, Inspector?'

'All I want to do is back up what's been said. Let's keep our eyes open and stay alert. We're all beginners as far as today's concerned, so we can't afford to be anything but one hundred per cent efficient. So good luck to all of us!'

Miles took a brief moment to cross to the Range Rover. Jill was in the passenger seat. She opened the door as he reached the vehicle.

'I wish you'd change your mind and let the others do it,' she said.

'You don't mean that.'

She nodded vigorously. 'Oh yes I do, Miles. I've only just got to know you and I don't like the thought of losing you.'

He leaned forward and kissed her. 'I wish we'd got up even earlier now,' he said, smiling as she actually blushed.

'I must admit I haven't ever enjoyed breakfast time so much as I did this morning.'

Miles took her hand in his. 'When we get in that mine I want you to stay inside here. Windows up and doors closed tight. In fact I wish you'd get away from here altogether.'

'No, Miles, I won't go. I'm staying put

until I see you come back out of that tunnel.'

Miles saw the firm set of her jaw. The stubborn gleam in her eyes and he knew better than to argue with her.

'I'll have to go.' He kissed her once more then hurried to join the others waiting near the tunnel entrance.

Sam Braddock nodded. 'All set?' he asked, his voice muffled behind the visor.

'Fine,' Miles said. He closed his own visor and led the way inside the tunnel.

Each man had a powerful lamp connected to his suit. As these were switched on strong shafts of light swept aside the dark shadows.

'Watch the sloping floor,' Miles called.

Rock crumbled under Miles's boots as he edged his way along the tunnel. His gaze was fixed on the rocky floor, eyes searching for signs that would prove the scorpions were using the mine. He wasn't surprised when he did see tell tale scuffs in the dust and dirt. There were other marks too — long trails that suggested something had been dragged along. And something else . . . two sets of bootprints heading *into* the mine. There were none coming out. He pointed this out to Braddock.

'Our missing students?' Braddock asked.

'It's what I was thinking.'

'Makes me wonder what else we're going to find.'

When they reached the gallery where the various subtunnels began Miles called a halt. He took a slow walk across the area. The only passage showing recent usage was the main one.

'I guess we take this one,' he said.

Sergeant McCabe indicated the smaller branches. 'If there's anything down any of those tunnels,' he pointed out, 'we could find ourselves cut off.'

'You're right,' Miles acknowledged. 'Do we leave someone here?'

'I think it would be the wisest thing to do,' McCabe said. 'One of my lads with a thrower and one other with a shotgun.'

Braddock glanced at his two men. 'Franklin, you stay here.'

As the two men stationed themselves the others moved on. They had only gone a couple of hundred yards when Miles raised his hand. Braddock, moving up to join him, saw the entomologist kneel down.

'Find something?'

Miles pointed to an object illuminated in the beam of his lamp. It was a decomposing human hand and section of forearm.

'And there,' Miles said, training his lamp a few yards further along. The object was a woman's shoe.

Miles stood up and they walked on. 'I have a feeling we're going to see more of that kind of thing.'

'Oh, you're a real barrel of laughs,' Braddock muttered dryly.

The rock walls were running with water now. It trickled along the floor, pooling wherever it could find a crevice.

'Christ, what's that stink?'

The question came from one of McCabe's men. The group drew to a halt as the overpowering stench reached them.

'How far do you reckon we've come?' Miles asked.

'Close on a quarter of a mile,' McCabe stated.

'Then we can't be far from the end of the tunnel.'

'Ranleigh. Over to your left,' Braddock said.

Miles allowed his lamplight to precede him as he turned. Some yards ahead, against the side of the tunnel, lay the dark shape of a scorpion. It was a large specimen. Over four feet in body length alone. Even as he saw it Miles realised they had nothing to fear from it. The creature was dead, its motionless body crusted with burst and dried sores.

'Jesus Christ!' someone whispered.

'No good calling on him,' came McCabe's bitter reply. 'He can't help us.'

'Is that the result of the infection they're carrying?' Braddock asked.

'Yes. Eventually it will simply overwhelm them and they'll die.'

'That one might be dead,' McCabe said quietly, 'but I'm bloody certain the one over to our right isn't!'

Miles turned. The beam from his lamp fell directly across the gleaming shape of a very live scorpion. The creature was scuttling towards them, tail up over its back, pincered arms jutting forward.

Miles swung up the shotgun, held the moving scorpion in his sights, and pulled back on the trigger. The explosion in the confines of the tunnel was terrific, sending shock-waves of sound rolling along the walls. The effect on the scorpion was devastating. It literally blew the creature apart. Ripped open the dark body in a spray of slimy pulp, knocking it yards back along the tunnel.

'We're committed now,' Miles said. 'Let's move!'

He ran forward, hampered by the bulky suit. He was sweating inside its heavy folds and a great deal of that sweat was from honest-to-goodness fear. Fear of what he might find up ahead of him, and also fear of what might happen to him if he made any mistakes.

The tunnel ahead curved round to the right, the floor starting to slope slightly. Miles noticed that it was also beginning to widen out. He recalled from what Richard Groves had told him that at the end of the main tunnel there was a large, natural cavern. The original engineers had discovered it during the creation of the mine. It had contained a large amount of the precious ore they were mining and sustained the mine for years. As the yield diminished the need for further tunnelling arose. No more tunnels were opened, however, because it was also at this time that the mine was closed down for good.

This information flashed through Miles's mind as he rounded the curve in the tunnel and saw before him the circular cavern that had once echoed to the sound of men clawing the valuable ore from its bowels. The cavern seethed with life once more. But this was a form of life never previously witnessed by man.

As the rest of the group caught up with Miles, halting at the edge of the cavern, their combined lamplight flooded the area before them, revealing a scene of horror totally alien to the human mind.

Scores of the creatures, startled by the brilliant light and the noise, were scuttling back and forth across the cavern floor.

'Am I really seeing it?' Braddock asked.

Miles nodded.

'Look!' yelled one of McCabe's men.

They all followed his pointing finger.

Strewn around the cavern floor, in various stages of decomposition and dismemberment, were dozens of human corpses. On the far side lay glistening mounds of sickly-white globes.

'Eggs!' Miles breathed. 'Hundreds of the damn things!'

'What do we do?' asked Braddock.

'Burn it!' Miles yelled. 'Burn it all!'

McCabe waved his men forward. 'You heard the man.'

'Make sure you destroy those eggs!' Miles said.

Tongues of fire spurted from the tips of the flame-throwers. The two soldiers edged forward, nervously eyeing the clustered mass of scorpions.

'Don't wait too long,' Miles warned. 'If those scorpions decide to move against us we're going to be knee-deep in the bloody things!'

The leading soldier decided he had little liking for that possibility. He raised the muzzle of his weapon and pressed the trigger. An ever-lengthening ribbon of liquid flame spewed from the nozzle, racing across the cavern. The brilliant glare threw elongated shadows onto the curved walls. The jet of fire scorched across the backs of the nearest scorpions, instantly transforming them into writhing balls of flame. As they curled up in agony, their bodies hissed and bubbled as their inner juices boiled out of them.

The second soldier eased to the far side and released a burst of hungry flame. It fell short of its intended target — the eggs. The soldier adjusted the angle of his nozzle and tried again. This time the eggs were engulfed in a seething mass of raw energy. The clinging, liquid fire devoured them as the soldier kept the nozzle steadily aimed.

'Ranleigh, I don't think those brutes are going to stand around much longer.' Braddock shouted a warning above the roar of the throwers.

'You're right, here they come!'

Even as he spoke the first of the scorpions broke from the main bunch and darted forward, closing in rapidly.

'Over here!' yelled Miles, swinging the muzzle of his shotgun round.

The scorpions were moving directly towards him. Miles wanted to turn and run — but he knew it was a foolish thought. The scorpions could easily outrun him. He stood his ground, easing back the shotgun's trigger. He held for as long as he dared before depressing it fully. The powerful blast killed three scorpions instantly, ripping their bodies apart. A fourth was badly injured; it squirmed on the floor, desperately trying to regain its balance on legs that no longer existed.

Braddock appeared at Miles's side. 'We're not going to hold them for long!' he said.

Miles simply nodded an acknowledgement. There was no time for anything else as the dark bodies began to emerge from the oily smoke. All he could do was trigger shot after shot at the advancing creatures.

The cavern echoed to the steady blast of shotguns as the others copied Miles's actions. It was a desperate attempt to buy time — time for the soldiers operating the flame-throwers to use their awful weapons to the best effect. As the dead scorpions began to litter the floor, they were engulfed by the curling tongues of flame.

'Mr Ranleigh!' McCabe yelled. He crossed to where Miles was standing and grabbed the entomologist's arm. 'Over here!'

Miles followed him. He peered through the visor of his suit, narrowing his eyes against the sweat that was trickling from his brow. As he identified the place McCabe was indicating a curse rose on his lips.

On the far side of the cavern, at a point where the rough side rose in a steep slope to a foot-wide ledge, a line of scorpions was moving swiftly to a dark fracture in the rock and vanishing from sight.

McCabe called to one of his men and showed him the spot. The soldier adjusted his flame-thrower and aimed a heavy tongue of flame at the fissure. It struck first time. The flame bounced back off the rock and engulfed a number of the scorpions moving up the ledge. Twisting and writhing they were burned to charred, skeletal shapes.

'What do you think?' McCabe asked. 'A way out for them?'

'Yes, I'm damn certain that's just what it . . .'

A frenzied scream cut through the general din.

'Ranleigh, look out!' Braddock yelled.

Miles turned and in the split second before Sam Braddock's hands struck him hard in the chest, he glimpsed a badly burned scorpion, its pincers clamped deep in the throat of a soldier wielding a flame-thrower. The man's frenzied fingers had jammed the trigger wide open and the nozzle belched a snaking lash of uncontrolled flame.

A stunning shock drove the breath from Miles's body as he hit the rock floor. The shotgun fell from his hand, and he felt the searing heat of flame as it burned bright before his eyes. The sweat dried on his body and his skin tightened, the roaring jet of fire seeming to hang over him for an eternity before fading away.

From a distance he heard raised voice. A hoarse rattle of a scream that rose and fell, dribbling away to silence. The sudden blast of a shotgun filled his ears.

Miles sat up, feeling a little foolish. He peered about him, thinking briefly that the cavern had taken on the aspect of some garish interpretation of hell. Curling tongues of flame rose from the twisted black shapes on the cavern floor and thick coils of smoke hovered uncertainly above the scene of carnage.

'You all right?'

Miles glanced at Sam Braddock. The policeman's protective suit was charred and streaked with soot.

'I'm fine. You?'

Braddock grinned. 'I'll survive.'

'Braddock — thanks.'

Miles picked up his shotgun and followed Braddock to where the others were standing over the soldier the scorpion had attacked. He lay on his back, eyes staring out through the blood splattered visor of his suit. The scorpion had ripped open the front of the suit and torn out the man's throat, savaging the flesh with maniacal ferocity. Shredded flesh and muscle, glistening with blood and mucus, had spilled down the front of the suit which was soaked to the waist.

Glancing in McCabe's direction Miles saw that the sergeant's face held a cold, hostile expression.

'Hey, I think some of them are still alive!' It was Braddock's constable who spoke.

Heads turned, eyes searching, trying to detect movement on the cavern floor. It was difficult. The drifting smoke tended to create the illusion of movement where there was none.

A faint tremor slithered along Miles's spine when he saw a number of dark shapes emerge from the smoke, rising on bristled legs.

'Over there,' he said, touching the arm of the soldier operating the flame-thrower.

'I see 'em,' the soldier said, edging forward.

'You stay where you are, Machin,' McCabe snapped. 'These bastards are mine!'

McCabe had removed the flame-thrower from the dead soldier. He had the tank unit in one hand and the nozzle in the other. Stepping in front of the rest of the group he walked forward so that he was directly in the path of the oncoming scorpions.

'McCabe, not so close!' Braddock warned.

The sergeant ignored him. He thrust the nozzle of the flame-thrower forward and pressed the trigger. It spat out a soft trickle of flame, died, then jetted out another.

'Sergeant — get rid of it!' screamed Machin.

An instant later there was a dull thump and McCabe was engulfed in a brilliant ball of flame. It boiled up and out, the heat causing the others to fall back — stunned by what was happening before their horrified gaze.

'A fucking blowback!' Machin yelled. 'Oh, Jesus Christ almighty!' He was almost weeping.

The fireball seemed to enlarge before its power waned, and only as it began to fade could McCabe's burning figure be seen. He was on the floor. A shrivelled, blistered, bubbling thing, pink strips of raw flesh peeling from his body as he writhed in agony.

Miles was jerked from his stunned trance only when a scorpion moved into his line of vision. The creature, picking up speed as it sensed Miles's awareness of its presence, came directly at him, tail arching menacingly over its back. Miles swung his shotgun up and fired. In his haste he missed. The charge kicked up a gout of dirt and the scorpion veered to one side. Miles fired again. This time the blast ripped the scorpion's head clean off. A gush of pulpy matter spewed from the gaping wound and the headless creature stumbled on for a few more feet before collapsing.

'Back to the tunnel,' Braddock ordered. 'Ranleigh, that means you, too!'

'We have to be sure they're all dead,' Miles argued.

'Don't worry,' Machin said. 'They'll all be dead!'

As the others moved to the tunnel Machin lagged behind. He faced the remaining scorpions, counting at least nine of the loathsome creatures. When he raised the nozzle of the flame-thrower they drew back, trying to decide whether or not to go any further.

'It's as if they know that flame-thrower's a threat to them,' Braddock said.

'I think they do,' Miles answered. 'It's why they're holding back.'

'You'll be telling me next they can talk to each other.'

'Some form of communication probably does exist. Extremely basic by our standards — but still communication.'

'I'll communicate with the bleeding things!' Machin said, and before anyone could speak he stepped forward. The nozzle of the flame-thrower spat flame and Machin began to hose the grouped scorpions. Caught in the clinging flame the creatures were instantly consumed. Hissing and popping they curled up and died without a chance of escape.

'Bastards!' Machin said forcibly as he stood and watched them burn.

Miles edged towards the perimeter and silently surveyed the scene. The cavern, misty with smoke and criss-crossed by the powerful beams of light from the lamps, was still. The floor was littered with dead scorpions and, at the far side, the egg crèches had been transformed into blackened mounds, melted by the intense heat.

Above his head a low grumble of sound attracted his attention. Miles glanced up to see a cascade of rock and dust shower down from the vaulted roof.

'I think we *had* better get out of here,' he snapped urgently.

Braddock, detecting the alarm in his tone, moved to his side. 'Problems?'

Miles indicated the still falling debris. 'We should have thought about that,' he said. 'All that shooting caused a hell of a lot of vibration in here. This place has been holding itself together for a long time.'

High overhead something shifted. A large chunk of crumbling rock smashed into fragments on the cavern floor.

'Machin, get back here, man!' Miles yelled.

Machin had heard the falling rock. He turned and ran as more debris began to shower from the roof. By some miracle Machin avoided being hit. He stumbled into the tunnel seconds before a massive fall of tons of rock and earth. Dust billowed up around the group and the walls began to shake.

'I suggest we get the hell out of here,' Miles said.

'Can you hear water?' Braddock asked.

'Water?'

They listened, and behind the tumbling clatter of falling rock could be heard the unmistakable noise of running water.

'Damn!' Miles exclaimed. 'That subterranean river! Weakening the blasted rock has given it a way in!'

'Now we have a choice,' Machin said. 'We can get squashed flat or bloody drowned!' He shrugged out of the flame-thrower harness and dropped the equipment on the ground. 'Well? What are we waiting for?'

'Go!' Miles yelled. 'Get out of here!'

They ran for their lives. Stumbling and banging against each other as they struggled up the sloping ground. Scraping against the rough walls, eyes peering through the misted visors of the suits. Trying to gauge what lay ahead in the dancing beams of lamp light. Around them the tunnel shook. Ancient wooden beams creaked and groaned as the rock they supported began to shift. Dirt and rubble rained down. The water began to flow steadily, spurting where it found weak spots in the walls.

From far back along the tunnel sound reached their ears: the thunder of a moving mass of water. Water that had gushed into the cavern was now seeking a fresh route. As each man became aware of what was happening the need for escape grew stronger.

Above their heads a heavy beam snapped, the tremendous pressure driving it downwards with the force of a power-ram. The jagged end of one section struck the shoulder of a running figure, splintered shards of wood ripping through weak flesh. The man went down screaming, the main section of the beam crushing his skull against the rock floor. Braddock paused long enough to play the beam of his lamp on the mess oozing from the sodden vizor of the man's protective suit to realise no help was needed.

Fear urged them on. Lungs burning

and hearts racing, they ignored the painful blows of the falling debris.

A cacophany of sound filled their ears, but above it all they could hear the roar of the underground river as it foamed its way into the tunnel, close behind them.

They burst out into the small gallery where the two backup men waited. Miles waved the others on and turned to the two startled figures. Unable to stand the constriction any longer he dragged the hood of the suit off his head and tossed it aside.

'No questions!' he yelled. 'Just get the hell out of here! Run! Now!'

He grabbed their arms and shoved them towards the exit tunnel.

Once again they ran. Leg muscles aching as they pushed themselves along the incline, trying to blot out the sound of the boiling flood at their heels.

They were within yards of escape when the surging mass of water overtook them. In an explosion of raw power it surged from the mouth of the tunnel, foaming white as it dissipated across the open ground beyond.

15

There was no going back. The dark, underground place that had provided shelter for so long was no more. Everything had gone. Food. The safety. The eggs so close to hatching. Destroyed. The security of the nest shattered . . .

The thirty surviving scorpions had emerged from the narrow fissure that had brought them from the deep cavern in to blazing sunlight. Utilising the wild terrain that surrounded them, they scattered and disappeared into the tangled undergrowth of High Moor.

They sought concealment, survival foremost in their thoughts. Many were in pain from the sickness ravaging their systems. The suffering increased their hostility which was directed towards their own kind and they engaged in savage bouts of violence, tearing and snapping at each other with unrestrained barbarity. Yet despite the wildness of these attacks, the deliberate brutality, no scorpion ever used the ultimate weapon on its adversary — the deadly stings remained retracted.

During the long hours of daylight the scorpions spread out across the wilderness of the moor, breaking off into small groups of twos and threes, sometimes more, while others chose a solitary path. Collective security seemed to have been abandoned.

Some sought shaded, hidden places where they could rest. For several it would be their last, their bodies unable to resist the increasing activity of the bacillus. They crawled into lonely places and died. Others searched for food. Survival was still the prime motivator — and survival meant nourishment.

High Moor was not completely deserted. It contained its own wildlife — though this was not enough to satisfy the needs of the scorpions. But in addition to the natural inhabitants there were the transient forms of life . . .

* * *

Benny Truscott raised his grizzled head and reluctantly opened one eye. Bright sunlight made him flinch. Somewhere far off he could hear the bleat of one of his sheep. The cry was indicative of distress. Benny sighed. The stupid thing had probably got itself tangled up in a bramble bush or something equally as senseless.

He reached for the stone flagon of scrumpy resting on the ground beside him. Raising it to his dry lips he took a long, slow swallow, savouring the bitter tang as the liquid coursed down his throat.

A second sheep started to bleat. Benny grumbled into his shaggy beard and sat upright, staring around. *Where the hell was Sam?* His dog was too good to allow *two* sheep to fall into trouble. Benny climbed to his feet, cursing softly. The flagon of scrumpy lay at his feet — forgotten.

The silent moor stretched out in all directions. Bright and hazy beneath the burnished blue curve of a cloudless sky. Nothing moved within Benny's line of vision.

Not even his flock of sheep!

Benny took off his battered old hat and used it to shade his eyes. A frown creased his brown face. *Where were the bloody things*? A whole flock of sheep didn't just up and vanish.

He walked along the ridge overlooking the slope. His keen eyes searched the undulating moorland. And his frown deepened. There wasn't a thing out there.

'*Sam*!' he yelled. His voice rolled out across the moor. It faded into silence. 'Come here, Sam! Here, Sam!'

Benny gripped the handle of his old walking stick so tight that his knuckles whitened. There was something strange going on.

Close by he heard faint bleating; a low, weak sound. Benny turned, and using his stick he parted the tangled undergrowth that blocked his path. Abruptly, the bush fell away behind him and he stood on the crest of the slope, the ground chopping away to a deep basin.

He spotted something in the grass and moved quickly forward. A moment later a low curse bubbled from his tight-set mouth.

Just a few feet ahead of him was Sam. On his side. His black and white coat streaked and soaked with blood. There was a lot more blood on the grass around him. It had come from the ragged hole that had once been the dog's neck. Some terrible force had ripped out the animal's throat, exposing bone and sinew. Sam's lips had peeled back in a final snarl of defiance. Blood had spilled from the part-open mouth, staining the gleaming teeth.

'Sam!' Benny whispered softly. He stood and stared at the dog, reluctant to accept what he was seeing.

Close by something disturbed the brush. Benny turned, peering into the tangle. Even as he watched the undergrowth parted and a scorpion lumbered into view. It held a large chunk of raw meat in one of its pincers. The meat was fresh and had bloodstained curly wool on one side.

Benny stared at the revolting thing. *It* seemed to be looking at him. Its cold eyes regarded him with suspicion. As it raised its head Benny could see its half-open mouth. Strings of flesh hung from it and blood dribbled freely onto the grass.

Benny couldn't put a name to the thing. Or understand what it was. He lived a solitary life up on the moor, having only minimal contact with the 'outside world' as he thought of it. He couldn't read, didn't own a radio or TV, and never bought newspapers. He knew nothing about scorpions.

For his sixty-two years he was an agile man — but if he'd been twenty-two his reflexes would not have provided the necessary impetus. His mind was still coming to terms with what his eyes were seeing. But his initial reaction was to turn and run. This thing — which had killed his dog and God knew how many of his sheep — was plainly ready to attack *him*.

In the time it took Benny to form the thought in his mind the scorpion attacked. There was no hesitation. No faltering. It darted forward, bloody pincers reaching out. They gripped and closed, rending flesh from bone, drawing blood. Benny was thrown backwards by the sheer ferocity of the attack. He lost his footing and fell heavily, twisting one arm beneath his body as he struck the ground. He cried out — once — the sound lost in the sickening crunch of bone. His right arm flopped uselessly at his side, splintered ends of bone protruding through the skin. As the dark, squirming thing crawled onto his chest, bringing with it the stench of its own rotting body, Benny struck out with his good hand. His clenched fist bounced off the hard body. For a moment he found himself staring into the jaws of the slavering scorpion. Then it dipped its head, the open mouth fastening on Benny's throat, the jagged teeth sinking into his soft flesh. Benny screamed, then began to choke as hot blood gushed into his mouth. Pain blurred his vision so he didn't see the pincered arm stretch over his head. The pincer remained poised for a few seconds and then dropped, the keen edges of the claws sliced into the top of his skull. Blood poured across his face, blinding him. Now he began to struggle. A frantic kicking born out of his abject fear of the nearness of death. His movements almost threw the scorpion from him. Somehow it clung fast and, without undue haste, arched forward its elongated tail, striking once with the glistening sting. As the powerful venom raced into Benny's bloodstream he lapsed into a deepening coma. His mind and body floated in eternal darkness.

The scorpion concentrated its efforts on the now limp body, tearing and ripping the juicy meat . . .

⋆ ⋆ ⋆

Ron Nash lowered the heavy binoculars, shaking his head wearily. He turned reluctantly and walked back to the silver and blue Range Rover parked by the side of the road. The vehicle belonged to Media News Inc. an international company which provided syndicated news items for television companies all over the world. Ron Nash and his team were the British-based unit. They had been in the west country, filming a documentary about the tourist industry versus the traditional ideals of the area, when one of

Nash's contacts — a clerk who worked in a government department in Whitehall — had passed along information that mutated scorpions had been sighted in the Port Pendall area. Government and local authorities were trying to suppress any news concerning the outbreak. They *were* trying — but not fully succeeding.

Nash, sensing a hot news story, had abandoned his documentary and despite the police and their roadblocks had taken his team into the area, using little-known, isolated lanes. He had worked his way round to High Moor — and he and his team had spent a fruitless morning combing the area.

'If these bloody scorpions exist they're keeping their heads down,' Vince Brooks said as Nash approached the Range Rover. Brooks was the cameraman. A tall, lean man with thinning hair and an almost invisible moustache across his upper lip.

Nash swung open the driver's door and reached for one of the mugs of hot coffee resting on the wide facia panel. He leaned against the side of the Rover and squinted up at the hot sky.

'When Dutton gave me the tip he told me that a team had already located the nest and destroyed it. It was in an abandoned tin mine. Some of the scorpions got out. Now, that mine was situated on the fringe of High Moor. Those things are here somewhere. I'm certain of it. This is the most logical place for them.'

From the rear seat came a soft chuckle. A broad-shouldered figure raised up from where it had been lying in the comparative shade. 'Since when have you been an expert on scorpions?'

'I missed out on that Long Point story,' Nash said. 'It was all over before I had a chance to get down to the place. I was bloody mad about that. I watched every item covering it. Read all the articles, too. And I learned a fair bit about scorpions. One of the things I remember is that they are, above everything else, dedicated survivors. Destroy their nest — they'll just go out and find a new one. Which is what they did in Long Point. And I think that's what they've done here. What Dutton told me fits the pattern. That team wiped out the scorpion nest. The ones that escaped will be looking for a new location. This moorland will offer them just what they're looking for. They're here. Somewhere on this moor. I'm bloody well certain!'

Tom Rowe, sound-recordist, leaned against the Rover's front seat. He yawned. Slowly and with great effort. 'Well if they are here I wish they'd show themselves. Christ, Ron, it's bloody dead up here!'

Brooks nodded in agreement. 'He's right, Ron. Can't we try further on?'

Nash didn't reply. He was staring over Brooks's shoulder, out across the moor. His eyes narrowed and he moved to the front of the Range Rover, raising the binoculars to his eyes.

'Ron?' Brooks stood beside him. 'You seen something?'

'Could be,' Nash said. 'Get your gear ready.'

Brooks snatched up his 35mm movie camera. Tom Rowe, humping a heavy portable tape-recorder, followed him.

'Sweet fucking Jesus!' Nash exclaimed, his voice full of excitement.

The others glanced at each other. It was unusual to hear Ron Nash express himself so volubly. He normally kept his emotions under tight control.

'Where?' asked Rowe.

Nash pointed across the undulating moorland. 'About two hundred yards out,' he said. His voice was trembling. 'Take a look.' He handed over the binoculars.

'He's right, Vince,' Rowe said a moment later. 'He's bloody right!'

Brooks lifted the 35mm camera and peered through the telephoto lens. After a few moments of seeing nothing but tangled brush his lens picked up movement. Brooks touched the camera's button and started filming.

A number of scorpions had appeared, dragging a large object across the rough ground.

'Ron, I'm sure that's a body,' Brooks said evenly, without breaking his filming.

Nash took the binoculars from Rowe and took another look himself. 'I think you're right. Come on, let's try and get in closer.'

The three men moved across the moor in the direction of the engrossed scorpions. As they got closer Nash could see that there were four of them. Despite his excitement he couldn't repress a shudder as he began to pick out details of the repulsive creatures. The dark, hard bodies. The cruel pincers that were ripping and shredding the flesh of the unfortunate victim. There was no mistaking the object now as a human body. Or what had been a human body. Practically naked and streaked with blood. One arm was missing. The stomach had been ripped open, exposing the glistening cavity beneath. A shocked groan escaped from Nash's lips as he saw one of the scorpions close its pincers over the corpse's skull. There was a sickly crunch and the top of the head was suddenly out of shape. The scorpion used the other set of pincers to tear away the flesh covering the skull. There was a rush of fluid and then a dark, soft mass swelled out of the open cavity.

'Oh Christ!' Tom Rowe moaned. He turned away, sagging to his knees, the heavy tape-recorder slipping from his shoulder as he bent his head and began to vomit.

Brooks, fighting against the nausea rising in his throat, kept his camera trained on the horrific scene. He stood his ground and watched the terrible event taking place before his stunned gaze.

A shrill scream rang out.

The sound came from Ron Nash. It came too late to save him. The yell was terminated seconds after a scorpion sank its sting in the side of his neck. Nash hadn't seen the creature emerge from the thick brush just behind him. He had only become aware of it a scant few seconds before it struck. The sting hurt. Like a badly inserted hypodermic needle. Almost instantly the powerful venom went to work. Paralysing him. Closing down all his sensory capabilities. Nash sank to the ground, unaware of anything except a spreading numbness. The day began to darken around him. Neither hot nor cold. He fell forward, face down, dying so quickly he didn't realise that the scorpion was frenziedly ripping the flesh from his bones.

As Nash's scream cut through the air Tom Rowe raised his head, sleeving sticky vomit from his mouth and chin. His frightened eyes settled on the scorpion savaging Nash's prostrate form. Rowe wrenched his head away, seeking Vince Brooks. The cameraman was still filming the scorpions tearing at the now almost unrecognisable corpse.

'Vince . . . ' Rowe screamed. He scrambled to his feet. Scared. Thrown off balance by the sudden shock. 'For fuck's sake, Vince, come on . . . '

The clustered scorpions were disturbed by Rowe's yelling. Their heads lifting in unison, dribbling blood, they searched for the source of the sound. The moment they set eyes on the men they turned away from the corpse and scuttled menacingly across the ground.

Brooks saw the move through the lens of his camera, and despite a reluctance to stop filming he realised that caution was the wisest course. He simply turned and ran. He passed Nash's sprawled body. A blood-spattered scorpion hunched over it, deadly pincers doing terrible things. Brooks ran on, trying to erase the image from his mind. The Range Rover seemed an endless distance away. He threw a desperate glance over his shoulder and saw that the scorpions were gaining. A sob burst from his lips as he stumbled, went down on one knee. As he fought to his feet he heard the scuttling rattle close behind him. He regained his balance, turning as he rose, and saw one of the creatures no more than a couple of feet away. It was reaching out with its snapping pincers, head up and mouth open. Brooks breathed in the evil stench. Saw the running sores oozing festering pus. His terror and building rage made him act without thought. As the scorpion lunged forward Brooks swung the heavy 35mm camera by its wrist strap, smashing it down on the scorpion's head. There was a wet sound. A sodden crunch. The head split wide open, pus bubbling from the gap. The scorpion collapsed instantly.

As Brooks continued his dash, he wondered briefly how Rowe was faring. He didn't look back. Despite his feelings for his friend he just daren't afford the time. And then he was at the Range Rover, clawing for the door handle. Hauling open the heavy door and throwing himself across the passenger seat. He heard something thud against the side of the vehicle. Felt it rock. He dragged the door shut. Again the impact of some solid object banging against the side. Turning his head he saw a black, glistening pincer appear above the lip of the door. It struck the window, glancing off.

Brooks slid across into the driving seat, fumbling for the ignition. He switched on and felt the powerful engine burst into life. Staring out through the window Brooks searched for Tom Rowe.

And saw him.

Rowe was stumbling, lurching drunkenly towards the road. A scorpion was clinging to his back like a horrible growth. Its legs gripping while its pincers snapped and tore. Rowe reached the road. He lost his footing and sprawled on the tarmac. His mouth was open in a continuous scream, though Brooks couldn't hear a sound above the roar of the engine. As Rowe fell the scorpion was dislodged. It landed on its back, legs windmilling frantically.

Brooks slammed the Rover into gear. He released the hand-brake and allowed the vehicle to leap forward. At the precise moment the scorpion regained its feet the Range Rover reached it. Brooks felt the left front wheel pass over the scorpion's body. He jammed on the brakes and brought the vehicle to a shuddering halt. Glancing back over his shoulder he saw that the remaining scorpions were holding back. Something had caused them to hesitate.

Pushing open the door Brooks climbed out and knelt beside Rowe. There seemed to be blood everywhere. Rowe's shirt was sodden with it. There was a large hole in the side of his neck, just below his left ear, the flesh chewed away to expose the neck muscles beneath. Brooks turned him over. Wide, staring eyes gazed off into some private distance. Rowe's mouth hung open. His breath came in shuddering rasps. Glancing over his shoulder

Brooks saw that the scorpions still hadn't moved. He took a deep breath, grasped Rowe under his arms and began to drag him to the waiting Rover. He unceremoniously dumped Rowe on the passenger seat, fastening the seat-belt across the limp form. Closing the door he made his cautious way round to his own seat. The scorpions remained where they were and Brooks kept the image in his rear mirror until it dwindled into nothing.

He drove along the coast road, following the signs to Port Pendall. He glanced at Rowe. The man was breathing with difficulty. His skin looked odd. Dark . . . Brooks just hoped that he could get to the hospital in time.

His foot hard down on the pedal, Brooks pushed the Range Rover to its limit, ignoring the speedometer's rising needle. His concentration was absorbed in keeping the speeding vehicle on the road. He was oblivious to everything else . . . including the police patrol car he passed. Minutes later the pulsing screech of its siren broke through to him. Brooks took a quick glance in the mirror, saw the patrol car with its flashing lights, and eased up on the pedal. There was no point in ignoring the police. In fact they could probably help him. He slowed and came to a stop at the side of the road.

'You do realise the speed you were going?' the uniformed constable said as he appeared at Brooks's window.

'I had a reason, officer,' Brooks said and indicated Tom Rowe's motionless figure. He was shocked himself to see how far the darkening of the skin had progressed.

'Where did it happen?' asked the constable; like the rest of the local force he had been told the kind of symptoms victims of the scorpions would exhibit.

'A few miles back along the road,' Brooks said. 'We were attacked by a number of scorpions. They killed one of our party and did this to Tom. Look, I'll tell you anything you need to know *after* I get to hospital.'

The constable nodded. 'Just follow us in.'

In under ten minutes they were driving through Port Pendall itself. The town was unusually quiet. The majority of holiday-makers had left. Some had stayed but were finding it hard to readjust to the abnormal calm of the place. The narrow streets and the harbour front, practically deserted, were not the same. They needed the jostling crowds. The noise and the colour. Port Pendall's tradespeople felt the departure of their customers more than most. They were geared to the frantic weeks of the season and the sudden exodus had left them in limbo. It gave them time to think. And the more they thought the angrier they became.

Brooks was unaware of this. He drove through Port Pendall with his eyes fixed firmly on the tail-lights of the police car and his mind on reaching the hospital. Nothing else mattered.

The town fell behind them. Brilliant greenery flashed by. Pale dust spumed up from the tyres of the police car as it drifted round a curve in the narrow road. A long straight lay ahead and then the low buildings of the hospital appeared. The police car swung off the road, the Range Rover following.

Brooks jammed on the brakes and the Range Rover slowed to a halt. Someone stepped forward and opened the passenger door. Gentle hands reached for Tom Rowe, unclipped the seat belt and lifted him down. Brooks watched as his friend was laid on a trolley and wheeled inside the accident unit.

'Thanks for your help,' Brooks said to the policeman.

'Just watch the speed next time,' the constable suggested as he got into the patrol car.

Brooks nodded absently. He could feel himself shivering slightly. Reaction, he decided. His body was slowing down after the high tension of the scorpion attack and then that wild car ride.

'Would you mind if I had a word?'

The question had to be repeated before Brooks heard it. He looked at the speaker and saw a slightly familiar figure — a tall man in his mid-thirties, with dark hair and a dark beard framing his tanned face.

'Are you all right?' Miles Ranleigh asked.

Brooks managed a weak grin. 'As long

as I don't have to move I'm fine.'

'Look — why don't you come inside. You'll get news of your friend as soon as there's any to give.'

'Sounds like a good idea.'

Miles led the way into the hospital and along the corridor to Richard Groves's office.

'Take a seat,' Miles said, crossing to where a percolater bubbled gently as it brewed fresh coffee. He filled a mug and handed it to Brooks.

Brooks took a long swallow. He leaned back and gazed at the ceiling.

'I never want to go through anything like that again,' he said.

'I know what you mean,' Miles sympathised.

Brooks glanced at him, almost ready to shout: *How the hell would you know*?

'I'm Miles Ranleigh.' Miles held out his hand. 'And I *do* know how you feel. I've been closer to those damn things than I ever wanted to be.'

Brooks dug deep into his mind and dragged out the almost-forgotten memory of where he'd heard Miles Ranleigh's name before. *Of course!* Ranleigh had been the entomologist involved in the scorpion scare at Long Point.

'Anything I can do to help?' Brooks asked.

Miles nodded. 'Could you pinpoint the location of the attack while it's still fresh in your mind?'

Miles handed him a map from the desk.

'We were here,' the cameraman said. He indicated the place on the map. 'Those damn things appeared out of nowhere. They were dragging a corpse along with them. We tried to get closer. Then another of the bloody things showed, and attacked Ron Nash. He was dead just like that. Next thing we knew the rest of the scorpions came after Tom and me.'

'You were lucky,' Miles said. He began to study the map.

'Any help?'

'You've confirmed a theory I've been developing.'

'Am I allowed to ask what it is?'

'Mmmm? Yes, of course.' Miles spread

the map flat on the top of the desk. 'In the three days since we destroyed the scorpions' nest in the abandoned mine there have been a number of incidents. Sightings of scorpions and actual attacks and deaths. All of them have been within a section of High Moor covering — roughly — this area.'

Brooks stared closely at the map. 'Do you think they've found themselves a new nest?'

'If they have we've been unable to spot it. Yesterday we even had police helicopters flying search-patterns over the moor. Didn't spot a thing.'

'Not exactly the ideal terrain for spotting things. I mean there's too much natural cover. All that brush. Grass. The uneven ground. There're enough places to hide a thousand scorpions.' Brooks smiled dryly: 'There *aren't* a thousand out there, of course?'

'That's the only thing we can be certain of,' Miles said. 'But as to the actual number — all we can do is guess.'

'And what's your estimate?'

'I'd say a couple of dozen. But don't

quote me on that.'

'So how do you stop them? If those things are hiding out on that moor isn't there the chance of them laying more eggs? Starting up another colony?'

'It's a possibility,' Miles agreed. 'We only have one thing working in our favour.'

'What's that?'

'The chance that an infection the scorpions are carrying will kill them off before they have the opportunity of setting up a new nest.'

'How long before that happens?'

'Now you're asking the one question I don't have an answer to. I just wish I did.'

'In the meantime?'

Miles tapped the map. 'All we can do is warn everyone to take care and keep up the patrols. It's a hit and miss arrangement — but it's all we have.'

16

Over the following three days the temperature rose to an all time high. Not a breath of wind ruffled the placid surface of Pendall Bay. The near-silent town itself shimmered uneasily beneath the cloudless, indifferent sky . . .

Sam Braddock's office was stuffy with heat. The odour of cigarette smoke and sweat hung heavily in the motionless air. Braddock himself, in his shirt-sleeves, sat behind his desk, confronted by six of Port Pendall's most influential businessmen. They were angry with him. Secretly Braddock was enjoying himself.

Roland Amberly, a large, overweight man of much wealth and incapable of seeing any further than the end of a pound note, leaned his bulk on his hands, which in turn were spread across the top of Braddock's desk.

'Just who are you trying to fool, Inspector? All this crap about swarms of wasps and summer insects is nothing but a smokescreen! It's just to hide the fact that you just don't know what to do about these bloody scorpions!'

'What scorpions?' Braddock asked. 'Have you been listening to rumours, Mr Amberly?'

'Oh come on, Inspector, we all know what's going on! I'm not without my own informants. Give me enough time and I'll tell you every secret in this town.'

'Mr Amberly, I couldn't care less about your grubby little schemes. The only thing that does concern me is the protection of the public. I'm old-fashioned enough to consider that part of my job. You believe what you like about the reports we've issued. If it achieves its ends then I'm satisfied.'

'All you've managed to do is drive away the tourists,' Amberly snapped. 'The tourists who keep this town alive during the summer season. And this is the best summer we've had for years. With a bloody deserted town! Damn you, Inspector, don't you realise the money we're losing?'

'I realise it means more to you than people and their lives.'

'Don't be so melodramatic — or pretend to be so naïve. Business is business, and I'm a businessman along with my colleagues. We have a right to know what you intend doing about this situation!'

'Nothing. The restriction on travel stays in force until I see fit to remove it. So do all the other restrictions.'

Amberly's florid face glistened with sweat. He stood upright and jabbed a thick finger in Braddock's face.

'You'll regret this, Inspector. I'm not without influence . . . '

'Don't tell me you have friends in high places, Mr Amberly.' Braddock suddenly slammed his fist down on the desk. 'Get out of my office, the lot of you — before I have you arrested for attempting to obstruct justice.'

Amberly and his group filed out of the office. At the door Amberly paused. 'This doesn't end here, Braddock,' he warned. 'I don't intend letting it end!'

On the pavement outside the police

station there was angry talk amongst the group. It ceased as Amberly forced his corpulent figure into the centre.

'I knew we were wasting our time,' he said. 'Well, the ball's in our court now. The only way we're going to get any action is to instigate it ourselves.'

'What do you have in mind?' someone asked.

Amberly smiled for the first time that day. 'First I want each one of you to contribute a signed cheque for cash. Then *I* am going to solve *our* problem!'

* * *

It was almost dark when Amberly eased the big car to a halt and sat staring through the windscreen at the derelict cottage. Now he had actually arrived he was experiencing a faint twinge of fear. He switched off the engine. It was very quiet. He'd had to drive almost a mile down a narrow overgrown lane to reach the cottage. It was the only building for miles around. He hadn't realised until now just how lonely a place this was. He pushed open the car door and climbed out. The night air was close and Amberly was sweating badly. The material of his trousers clung uncomfortably to the flabby insides of his thighs. He closed the car door and walked towards the cottage.

In the semi-darkness he stumbled, his feet catching unseen objects littering the ground. Amberly swore under his breath. *What a bloody awful place this was*. He breathed a sigh of relief as he reached the front door. Raised his hand to knock . . .

The door opened abruptly. Light spilled from the room beyond, casting a yellow pallor over Amberly's sweaty face. He found himself face to face with a broad-shouldered young man clad in stained denims and a tattered leather jacket. The man's hair hung in matted strings, reaching the collar of his jacket.

'Amberly?' he asked.

'Yes.'

The man stepped aside. 'Come on in, man.'

Stepping through the door Amberly breathed in the cloying stench of the room. It was a mixture of sweat and oil and sweetish smoke. Amberly took off his hat, wiping a hand across his sticky forehead.

The room was inadequately lit by an oil-lamp. Amberly could make out the jumble of scattered furniture and personal belongings. In the stone fireplace a fire burned and cooking utensils lay on the hearth.

Aware of being watched, Amberly peered into the shadows and one by one discerned the silent figures staring at him with unconcealed hostility. There were eight of them. He later realised that three were women. In the beginning it was hard to tell the difference because they were all dressed alike in the universal uniform of the young. Denims in various stages of disintegration. Leather jackets. Sweat-shirts. Leather boots. Male and female alike sported long, unkempt hair. *They were*, Amberly decided instantly, *a bunch of useless layabouts*. However he was going to have to keep his opinions to himself because they were going to be very useful to him.

The door banged shut and the man

who had let him in came to face him.

'Right, man,' he said, in the sub-dialect culled from countless American movies. 'Lay the deal on me.'

Amberly restrained an amused smile. 'How much did Con Regan tell you?'

'Listen, man, I'm Jack Talon. I don't deal with the hired help. This is my bunch and *I* tell them what to do. You and me, we rap, then I tell them.'

'All right, Talon, let's talk,' Amberly said.

Talon led him to the far side of the room. 'So?'

'Regan tells me you're not scared of anything. Is that true?'

'What's to be scared of, man? Hell, we're all going to snuff it one day. Maybe we'll all get crisped if somebody fingers the button and the bomb drops. Think about that and there ain't much else to get wet pants over.'

'What about these giant scorpions we have in the area?'

Talon grinned. 'Wild, man. It's crazy. Oversized insects. That's science for you, man. Like everything else in this fucking world. People are just screwing it up.'

Talon fell silent for a moment. 'What are they to you, man?'

'To put it bluntly, Talon, they're a pain in the arse! As long as they're around the tourists are going to stay away. And every day they do it costs me and my associates money.'

A knowing gleam entered Talon's eyes. 'Hell, man, you're what the Reds would call a decadent capitalist. Looking to protect the almighty pound.'

'I don't deny it,' Amberly said. 'Are you against money, Talon?'

'Me? Against money? Shit, man, what do you think I am, a frigging asshole?'

'I thought we'd have a common interest,' Amberly said. 'Now how would you and your people like to earn some?'

Talon frowned. 'Careful how you phrase that, man. Just the thought of working could cause some of them to pass out. What I have to do is make it sound like we're doing something for the hell of it. The money can be a bonus.'

'It will be more than a bonus, Talon.'

'Big bread, huh?' Talon leaned forward. 'How big?'

'My associates and I have all contributed. I'm talking money in the region of a couple of thousand pounds!'

Talon cleared his throat. 'You serious, man?' He saw that Amberly was. 'What do we have to do to make it?'

'The scorpions which escaped from the abandoned mine appear to have made the moor their new home. The police aren't having much success at getting rid of them. They're too cautious. Too concerned with procedure and downright bloodymindedness. It's fine for them to take their time. I can't afford to wait. I want action and I want it now. The money I'm offering, Talon, is yours when those scorpions are destroyed.'

'Ain't going to be easy, man.'

'Can't you do it?'

Talon raised a hand. 'Hold on, man, I didn't say that. Hell, I ain't scared of a few big bugs. We'll get rid of 'em for you. Just needs a little figuring how to do it.'

'I can supply you with anything you need,' Amberly offered. 'Tell me what you want. Guns? I can get them. There won't be any licences to go with them, though.

If the police find you with them . . . '

'Let me worry about the fuzz, man. They don't bother me. But I'll take your offer. Some shotguns would do the trick. Automatic pump-action.'

'I'll arrange it.'

'When can you get 'em?'

'In the morning.'

'You do that, man, and your troubles are over,' Talon said. 'Hey, what about petrol for our bikes? We're going to need full tanks, man.'

'You know the filling station just outside town? The Shell one? Be there at ten o'clock in the morning and you'll have your petrol and the guns.'

Talon chuckled. 'A tiger in the tank and a scorpion on our tails! Man, it's going to be a breeze!' He fell silent, a shrewd expression in his eyes now. 'What about a down-payment, man? I mean, you could be ripping us off?'

Amberly shook his head. 'Do you think I'd try to cheat someone like you, Talon? I may not be 'hip' but I'm not stupid either.' He reached inside his coat and took out a manila envelope. From it he took a thick wad of banknotes. He held it out to Talon. 'Five hundred pounds, Talon. Just to show my faith in you. Do the job right and there will be fifteen hundred more for you. It's a lot of money, Talon. It can buy you a lot of things.'

Talon took the money. He ran his fingers along the edge of the thick wad. 'Amberly, for once we're speaking the same language!'

'I knew we'd get along, Talon. I just knew it.'

17

‘*Fluorescence!*’

Jill, on her way from the kitchen with a tray holding cups and a pot of fresh coffee, glanced over to where Miles was perched on the couch. He was surrounded by opened reference books.

‘What did you say?’

He looked up, grinning. ‘I could kick myself,’ he said. ‘I’ve been too close to the trees to see the wood.’

‘I’d like a translation.’

‘Scorpions are prone to fluorescence. Shine an ultra-violet light on them and they give off a luminous glow.’ Miles closed the book he was holding with a bang. ‘Nature’s provided us with a solution and I almost overlooked it.’

‘This ultra-violet light would show them up even if they were in dense undergrowth?’

‘Enough for us to spot them. And any nests they might be building.’

Jill pushed a pile of books aside and sat down beside him. 'This could help you destroy them?'

'It gives us a chance. The break we need.'

'Here, have a cup of coffee before you get too excited.' Jill placed the tray on the coffee table and poured out a cup of black coffee. 'Miles, you should take some time off now. Try and relax. You look worn out. You've hardly been off your feet for the past few days. If you haven't been out with Sam Braddock you've been at the hospital. And even when you've managed to get back here it's only been to stick your nose in these damn books.'

'I suppose I have been rotten company,' Miles said.

'That wasn't what I meant. Miles, you took a nasty battering in that mine. All of you did. And instead of resting you all started chasing about the countryside searching for scorpions. Risking your lives every minute of the day.'

'Somebody has to do it, Jill. And we have managed to kill off a few of the things. But we all knew a few aren't enough. We need to destroy them all. That's why I've been doing all this reading. Trying to find a way that would give us an edge. Now I've found it.'

Miles reached for the phone and dialled Sam Braddock's home number. 'Braddock? This is Miles Ranleigh. Listen, I've found a way to spot the scorpions. We'll need your helicopters again and some special equipment.' He briefly explained what he needed.

'It'll take some time to organise,' Braddock said. 'I'll get in touch with a couple of my contacts. See what they can do. Come down to the station in the morning and I'll give you a progress report.'

'All right.'

'Goodnight, Ranleigh, and thanks.'

Miles replaced the receiver.

'Right,' Jill said determinedly. 'No more work tonight, Mr Ranleigh. As of now you are off duty.'

Leaning back on the couch Miles drank his coffee, admitting that it was pleasant being able to relax. He closed his eyes — just for a moment — and knew no more until he woke late the following morning. He opened his eyes to bright sunlight streaming in through the window of Jill's bedroom. As he slowly roused himself he realised he was alone in the large, comfortable bed.

'Hi!'

Miles turned his head and saw Jill coming in through the bedroom door. She wore a smile on her lovely face and nothing else. Drowsy as he was Miles found it difficult to concentrate on anything except her lithe, tanned body.

'What time is it?' he asked in an attempt to divert his attention.

'Around eleven-thirty,' Jill said, adding quickly: 'And before you leap out of bed — I called the Inspector ages ago and told him you were catching up on some badly needed sleep. He agreed with me and said to tell you there's no need to panic because the ultra-violet lights won't be available until late this afternoon. The police workshops will fit them and Braddock expects the 'copters to be ready by midday tomorrow.' Jill perched herself on the edge of the bed. 'So relax.'

Miles flopped back on the pillow. 'You've got it all worked out. By the way — how did I get up here last night? And where are my clothes?'

Jill grinned. '*I* brought you up. Practically had to carry you.' She leaned towards him. 'As for your clothes. Well you didn't take them off yourself . . . so I must have.'

'I've heard about women like you — getting your kicks by all manner of perverse acts.'

Jill lowered herself against him, breasts warm against his chest. 'I like my kicks straight,' she murmured. 'Or have you forgotten?'

'No,' he said. 'So why don't we get this damn sheet out of the way so you can demonstrate.'

She lowered her mouth to his, sliding her hand down his body, across his taut stomach. Her fingers curled around the rising length of his penis, teasing it gently. Miles responded to her touch, his aching shaft hardening rapidly, thrusting stiffly erect in her hand. Jill twisted against him, her free hand pulling away the offending barrier of the sheet. Her long, curving thighs spread sensuously as Miles laid his hand on the dark crown of hair at their junction. His searching fingers located the slippery opening of her vagina. Her soft whisper of excitement spurred him on and he probed deeper, gently moving his fingers inside her.

'Miles . . . please . . . now . . . ' she moaned. Her body was tensed, curving like a drawn bow.

He rolled between her open legs, feeling her fingers guide him to her moist lips. The softness closed over the sensitive tip of his penis, and he thrust his way in, penetrating deeply. Jill released a long sigh. Her warm flesh enfolded him, hips lifting to match his strokes. Miles held her, listening to the frantic breathing that was as much his own as hers, and lost himself in the race that would only end when each had satisfied their primal urges . . .

The food on the breakfast tray had gone cold. They both stared at the congealed mess. Miles touched the pot of coffee; that was cold as well.

'I'll go and cook some more,' Jill said. 'I'm starving.'

'Me too,' Miles said.

'Give me five minutes to shower.'

'I'll join you.'

She laughed as she swung her legs off the bed. 'Oh no, you don't! If I let you join me in the shower we'll still be in there at midnight!' At the bathroom door she turned. 'Go for yours when I'm downstairs. Preferably a *cold* shower!'

Half an hour later Miles went downstairs. The long shower had freshened him completely, and it hadn't been a cold one. He'd put on clean clothes as well. He paused at the bottom of the stairs as he caught a whiff of the cooking smells emanating from the kitchen.

'Do you mind ham and eggs?' Jill asked. 'It's that or nothing.'

'Ham and eggs sounds fine. Couple of eggs for me, please.'

'Ready in a minute.'

'Okay.'

Miles picked up the phone and dialled the Port Pendall police station.

'I'm sorry, Mr Ranleigh, but Inspector

Braddock's out at the moment. Something to do with the special equipment you want. He expects to be back in an hour or so.'

'Thanks. I'll call later.'

'Everything all right?' Jill asked.

'Far as I know. Braddock's out chasing those ultra-violet lights.'

'Sit down and eat then!' Jill placed a plate in front of him. 'You need your energy restoring.'

'Seems I recall you used a fair amount yourself.'

'Well I never was one for spectator sports.'

'You're looking more relaxed,' Jill observed later, over coffee.

'I feel it. You were right — I needed a break.'

'Make the most of it. I have a feeling you'll be busy tomorrow.'

18

The silence of the moor was shattered by the pulsing roar of powerful motorcycle engines. Nine gleaming machines rolled effortlessly across the undulating landscape, weaving in and out of the tangled brush. They trailed across the moor in the afternoon sun, stopping only when the lead rider raised his hand.

Jack Talon glanced over his shoulder and watched the rest of the riders bring their machines to a stop. He reached up and adjusted the sling holding the shotgun across his back. *Had to hand it to that feller Amberly. He'd promised guns and he'd delivered.* Talon grinned as he thought about the rest of the money Amberly had offered. *Fifteen hundred pounds!* That kind of money could keep them rolling for months.

''Hey, Talon, what now?'

'We find us some scorpions, Bike, and blow 'em to hell!'

Bike pushed his peaked cap to the back of his head. 'How? Whistle 'em up?'

A ripple of laughter rolled around the group.

'*They'll* find us,' Talon said.

'That's what I'm worried about,' Bike said.

One of the girls spoke up. 'Isn't this where those newsmen were attacked?' Junie, a tall, striking blonde with an aggressive manner, allowed her unease to show through her usually tough exterior. 'Makes me wonder if we really need all that money.'

'Of course we need it. How often do we get a chance at big money like that?'

'If we end up dead it isn't going to do us much good!'

'What's with you, Junie? Gettin' scared?'

'Yes.'

'Well cool it, baby, cause this is going to be a breeze.'

'Hey, Jack, what if the fuzz shows?'

'The cops can't be everywhere, Chopper,' Talon said. He glanced round the rest of the group. 'What's wrong with you assholes?'

‘We ain’t done nothin’ like this before, Talon,’ Bike said. ‘This ain’t the same as beating up some creeps in a pub yard.’

Talon banged his fist against the side of his bike’s petrol tank. ‘Jesus fucking Christ! A whole damn bunch of assholes. I reckon you bastards are all getting soft! Soft as shit!’

‘I don’t have to take that kind of crap,’ Chopper yelled angrily.

As they moved closer the rest of the group sensed another clash of personalities. Chopper never made any attempt to conceal the fact that he considered himself a better man than Talon.

‘As long as I’m running this bunch I say what I want,’ Talon yelled.

Chopper stepped away from his bike, his unshaven face twisted with uncontrolled anger. ‘You bastard! I’ll show you . . . ’

Junie’s scream interrupted the confrontation.

Everyone turned.

Silently. Swiftly. With the inborn cunning that was part of their make up, the scorpions had come. Eight of them.

Forming a ragged half-circle and moving towards the group with measured deliberation . . .

'Chopper — you still want to argue?' Talon asked.

Chopper raised two fingers at him before running to his bike and mounting it.

Sensing a temporary victory Talon turned to face the scorpions. *Christ, but they're fucking ugly*!

Chopper brought his machine round to face the line of scorpions and opened the throttle wide. He was yelling something, the sound lost in the bellow of the bike's exhaust. The bike leapt forward spraying a fountain of dirt and moss. Chopper drove one-handed, the other levelled the muzzle of the shotgun, the butt jammed against his hip. He rode straight at the scorpions, holding his fire until the last moment. Then the shotgun spat a gout of flame and smoke.

The charge caught one scorpion between the eyes, ripping its head open in a mushroom of spray.

Chopper's yell of triumph rose above

everything else. And then his bike, twisted off-course by the recoil of the shotgun, slewed to one side, rear wheel spinning as it lost contact with the ground. He tried to right the skid. He was too late. The bike slid from under him, throwing its rider to the ground. He rolled over a few times, then climbed groggily to his feet, shaking his head.

'Chopper, look out!' somebody yelled.

Chopper raised his head. Too late for him to do anything but stare in horror at the scorpion that had already begun its attack.

To those watching it seemed only as if the scorpion had made a casual gesture with its clawed arm. Chopper stepped back, half turning. A splash of red misted the air just above his waist. As Chopper continued to turn the red mist expanded and a multi-coloured streamer spilled from it, trailing gently to the ground.

'Jesus!' Talon moaned.

Chopper sank to his knees, his body collapsing like a deflated balloon as he followed the streamer — his own entrails — to the ground. He was clutching his hands over the gaping hole in his stomach. They were drenched in blood. It poured from his body in a flood.

'All right — what are we waiting for!' Talon screamed. 'Let's get the bastards!'

He ran forward, raising his shotgun and firing at the closest scorpion. Despite his previous bragging, he was *not* all that conversant with firearms. His shot missed, simply lifting a geyser of earth into the air. Talon hurriedly worked the shotgun's reload mechanism. In his haste he slammed the slide back clumsily and managed to jam it. Realising what he'd done Talon panicked and in his desperation kept on running towards the scorpions.

Alarmed by the noise and the destructive power of the shotguns, they reacted instantly. Jack Talon let out a frenzied scream as something tore deep into his left thigh. Pain spread up his leg, burning to the bone. He tried to tear himself free, but only added to the pain. The white-hot sear of agony intensified as his thigh bone was crushed. He screamed. The pressure increased and the bone began to splinter.

Talon struggled, losing his balance in the process. He fell to the ground and found himself staring into the eyes of the scorpion that had his leg gripped in one of its claws. A sickly stench issued from the creature. Its hard body-shell had cracked in a number of places, allowing a foul pus to escape. Talon made another attempt to free himself. A shriek of agony was wrenched from his lips as the scorpion fully closed its claw. Blood spurted thickly from the wound.

The creature edged forward, extending the other arm. The claw snapped at Talon's face, stripping a layer of flesh from his left cheek. Talon jerked his head back, conscious of the blood streaming down his face and neck. He saw the bloody claw reaching out again. Felt the briefly numbing shock as it again snatched at his face. There was a ripping sensation as the serrated edge severed tissue, muscle and stringy tendons, dragging his left eye from its socket, exposing his gums and teeth. The pain tore at his very soul. Talon screamed wildly. He felt blood pulsing from the great wound, filling his mouth and throat so that he began to choke. He was barely aware of the scorpion as it crawled across his body. His only response was a final, agonised arching of his spine as the creature dipped its head and sank its teeth into his exposed throat.

The eventual death of their leader went unnoticed by the rest of his group. They were too busy fighting for their own lives. In the minutes that followed there was mass slaughter as the scorpions encircled and attacked the confused, panicking humans. The shotguns, so willingly supplied by Roland Amberly, were hardly used. There was no time and few of the group had ever used such weapons; the boot and the broken bottle were more familiar. Suddenly they were surrounded by the nightmare creatures; only this was no nightmare. It was real and it was happening to them. They were being hurt. Bleeding. Screaming. And dying.

Bike, his face smeared with blood, and his left arm laid open to the bone, somehow freed himself from the grip of a slavering scorpion. On his feet, ignoring the cries for help from his friends, he lunged for his motorcycle. It was still on its stand, engine ticking over quietly. Bike threw himself across the saddle, swinging his leg over the machine. His hands reached for the grips, ready to guide the machine away from the scene of bloody slaughter.

It was as far as he got.

No more than a few yards away, another member of the group, fighting insanely to free himself, wrenched the shotgun he was holding up towards the scorpion. He jammed the muzzle against the creature's body and pulled the trigger. The point-blank charge ripped the scorpion in half, tossing its pulped remains across the ground. Sobbing in triumph the freed victim worked another cartridge into the shotgun's breech before scrambling up off the ground. He was unaware that during the terrible struggle with the attacking scorpions the creature had clawed at his right leg, just above the ankle. The flesh had been stripped to the bone and the tendons badly mauled. Now, as weight was put on the foot, blood pumped out of the gnawed flesh. Pain flashed up the limb. The foot refused to support the weight of the body . . . and the man plunged face down. As he struck the ground, his finger jerked back on the trigger of the shotgun. The weapon exploded with a roar. The concentrated blast of the shot struck Bike's machine, ripping a ragged hole in the petrol tank and taking off Bike's left knee in a bloody splash. The petrol tank was full and the raw fuel gushed from the hole. It spilled onto the hot exhaust pipe and there was a dull thump as the petrol flared, spread, then blazed into a fiery ball. Bike was engulfed in flame, his clothing catching fire quickly. He tumbled to the ground, thrashing wildly.

As the blazing petrol spread out across the ground the dry moss and scrub growth caught swiftly. The flames darted eagerly through the vegetation. There was nothing to stop it. There hadn't been a drop of rain for weeks.

The scorpions were the first to draw away. Fire terrified them. Through the ages it had always been the invincible foe.

And despite their new strength, their size, the scorpions were still powerless against it. A number of them were trapped by the rising flames. They fought to the last. Defying the searing heat, the hungry tongues of fire that shrivelled and blistered their bodies until they curled up and died.

The fire raced across the moor with terrifying speed. It spread in all directions, devouring the dry undergrowth, reaching ever outwards. Flames rose to the shimmering sky and swirling smoke billowed high into the air.

Every kind of living creature on the moor ran from the flames. It was out of control. Threatening to engulf the entire moor. They all ran. The moor's natural wildlife. And the two-legged invaders.

And the scorpions.

They all ran. Escaping from the flames. Searching for a safer place . . .

19

Fire appliances were brought in from as far away as Penzance to assist in the futile attempts to quell the High Moor blaze. The fire had gained a hold long before the first unit arrived from Port Pendall. Roaring flames were leaping across acres of open moorland, greedily engulfing the dry vegetation.

It was swiftly realised that all that could be done was to contain the blaze. The main concern was to stop it reaching Port Pendall. The moor ran out close to the town but there was enough woodland and combustible material around for flames to reach buildings on the outskirts. It was decided to concentrate the strength of the fire services close to Port Pendall, to create firebreaks that might hold back the mass of flames. Fire appliances were stationed in the vicinity, ready to deal with any fire managing to breach the fire-breaks. Port Pendall found itself threatened once again.

* * *

From his seat in the police helicopter Miles Ranleigh looked down on the raging inferno that had been High Moor. The helicopter pilot was having to maintain a high altitude to keep above the dense clouds of smoke rising from the blaze. The heat was also causing slight turbulence as super-heated air rose above the flames.

Miles turned to Sam Braddock. The policeman was staring out of his window, shaking his head as he surveyed the chaos on the ground below.

'Bloody typical,' he grumbled. 'Look at all those tourists jamming the roads. They ran like hell when they got the scorpion scare. Now they're back just to have a look at a bloody fire.' He slumped back in his seat. 'Ranleigh, if I live to be a hundred I'll never figure out what makes people tick.'

'Don't try,' Miles said. 'Man is the most complex life-form there is. There's no logical reasoning to half his actions. The human species has the capability to create marvels. To express compassion. To take his species to the finest limits. But he is also capable of the basest, most brutal outrages imaginable. How can you come to terms with a creature like that?' He gave a slight smile. 'Why do you think I chose entomology? Insects are a lot easier to understand.'

'Like your scorpions, I suppose?'

'Hey, not so much of the *your* scorpions. But I can well understand their actions. Right now they're trying to come to terms with a change in their physical and mental make up. They feel threatened — which they are. They also feel confused and that confusion will have been increased because of the disease that is slowly killing them. In a situation like that they react in the normal way of the scorpion. They strike out at whatever they consider their enemy. And I think that by now they have established us as their enemy. Every major contact we've had with them has been because of our attempts to destroy them. Exactly the same happened before this fire. That gang of morons was hired simply to seek out the scorpions and eliminate them. Instead the scorpions did the eliminating. Those three kids who were dragged out of the fire were lucky — if you can call being half-roasted lucky.'

'I'd like to hang the lot of them,' Braddock grumbled.

'In a way they may have done us a favour, Inspector.'

'A *favour*? Haven't you noticed that inferno down there?'

'Yes, I have. And also the fact that it's burning everything in its path. Which hopefully will include any and all dead scorpions. Any too sick to get away. Plus any eggs which may have been laid. It'll also save us the bother of carrying through the fluorescent idea.'

'What about the ones that manage to avoid the fire? They're going to go to ground somewhere.'

'There aren't many ways left open to them,' Miles said. 'The sea on one side and the fire moving along *and* across the moor. Like it or not, Inspector, they'll be driven towards town.'

'That's what I was afraid of. More than anything I'm concerned about the disease they're carrying. People dead from stinging or being clawed to death — that's one thing. But if enough people become infected by that disease we could end up with a fullscale epidemic on our hands. I haven't forgotten what young Parkinson looked like when they found him.'

'Richard Groves and his team are still working on an effective vaccine,' Miles said. 'The trouble is they're having problems establishing a basis from which they can develop it.'

'Which means they need time. The one thing we haven't got.'

* * *

The sign read: ROAD CLOSED. POLICE NOTICE. It was bolted to a metal frame designed so that it could be placed easily across a road, blocking it off. Two uniformed firemen had manhandled the unit out of the Fire Department Land Rover and were in the act of placing it in the road.

'Wish we could have some wind,' Stan Brewer said. 'Smoke from that blaze keeps drifting down here. My eyes feel like two piss 'oles in the snow.'

Len Grover smiled. 'Your eyes always look like piss 'oles in the snow.'

Stan stood upright. He leaned against the metal stand of the notice board. 'Bugger it, I'm 'avin' a minute.'

'I'll join you.'

Behind them, a mile or so away, the burning moor sent flame and smoke billowing skyward.

Len sleeved sweat from his flushed face. He was a big man. Heavy, and he hated hot weather.

'Hey, Len, what do we do if we meet up with any of them scorpions?' Stan asked, grinning easily.

'Run!' Len said shortly. He felt suddenly uneasy, wishing that Stan hadn't mentioned them. He was nervous enough without him asking bloody daft questions. It made him sick just thinking about the scorpions.

'I'd like to see that,' Stan said. 'You — running.'

Len began to reply. He decided against it. It was too hot to argue. Stan had a wicked sense of humour and once he knew he'd got someone rattled he would keep on at them.

'Let's get the rest of these bloody signs done!' he said, and turned back towards the Land Rover.

'Be with you in a minute,' Stan said. 'I've got to 'ave a pee 'fore I burst.'

He made his way towards the grass verge edging the road.

Len walked to the Land Rover. He climbed behind the wheel, grumbling as his sweaty shirt stuck damply to his back. He stared out through the fly-spattered windscreen, gazing up at the brassy blue sky.

'Rain for Christ's sake,' he muttered. 'Let's have some rain!'

In the far distance he could hear the muted roar of the fire. Closer he picked up the hum of insects hovering above the tall grass edging the road. The near silence, combined with the cloying heat, made Len drowsy. Almost without being aware he leaned against the back of the seat. His eyelids drooped. His breathing became low and steady.

He sat upright with a jerk. Stared about him guiltily. Len rubbed his face with his hands. His head was aching slightly. Glancing at his watch he saw that almost twenty minutes had gone by. *Where the hell was Stan?* It didn't take twenty minutes to have a . . .

Len opened the door and eased out of the Land Rover. He stood beside the vehicle for a moment, hesitant now he was outside its protection. He felt extremely vunerable. And he was unable to forget about the scorpions. They could be close by now. Lurking in the long grass beside the road. *What if they were watching him?* Len licked his dry lips. He was beginning to feel sick. Len had never considered whether he was a brave man or a coward. He admitted he was frightened now. Mainly because he wasn't certain what he might be facing.

He edged away from the Land Rover, moving towards the side of the narrow road. The grass verge dropped away in a shallow slope from the edge, so he couldn't see whether Stan was still there or not.

As he reached the top of the slope and looked into the shallow ditch a strangled sob rose in his throat.

The sound attracted the attention of the scorpion that was straddling Stan's sprawled body. It raised its head, eyes settling on Len. Blood dribbled freely from its glistening mouth. One claw was clamped tightly around Stan's shredded neck, lifting him slightly off the ground so that his head hung limply. Strips of raw, fatty flesh hung down from Stan's cheeks . . .

'Oh God!' Len muttered.

He stared at the awful sight for what seemed a long time. He was shocked. His senses recoiling. He stumbled away from the grass verge, boots rapping against the tarmac. He had to get to the Land Rover. Use the radio to call for help . . . he stopped dead in his tracks.

A second scorpion was squatting in the road, between him and the Land Rover. It looked far larger than the one he'd just seen. And its body was covered in running sores. One of its eyes was covered by a milky film.

The scorpion's curving tail rolled forward over its back. Len could see the glistening sting at the tip. He shuddered. Any minute now he was going to wet himself. The scorpion scuttled forward suddenly. No warning. It simply came at him.

At almost the last moment Len remembered the hand-axe on his belt. Standard equipment for members of the fire service. He unsnapped the flap of the pouch and snatched the axe free. He threw his body sideways, in an ungraceful movement. He fell, hitting the surface of the road hard. The impact knocked the breath from his body. Struggling for air like a drowning man, Len twisted his head to look over his shoulder. A claw slashed at his body. Len yelled in fright as he felt the tip tear the sleeve of his shirt and gouge the flesh of his upper arm.

Hurt and angry he struck out with the axe. The keen blade sliced home just above the claw. Len felt the blade sink in. He pulled it free and struck a second time. The fine honed blade cut through the arm, severing the claw. The scorpion drew back, mouth opening in a grimace of rage. Len dragged himself away from the scorpion, scrambling to his feet and running to the Land Rover. As he fell inside he heard the dry rattle of the scorpion scuttling along the road. It struck the side of the Land Rover hard, rocking the vehicle. Len tried to ignore it as he turned on the ignition, moving the key all the way. The Land Rover's engine burst into life. Len slapped it into gear and jammed his foot hard down. Tyres screeched, leaving a black burn mark on the surface. Len fought to hold the wheel as the Land Rover juddered and lurched along the road. Len imagined he was free from the scorpion threat.

He was wrong.

Very wrong.

It was Len's last mistake, because it was one which lost him his life.

Len hadn't noticed the scorpion that had secreted itself in the pile of equipment in the vehicle's rear. His first indication of its presence was the cruel claw that snapped into the back of his neck. Len felt the flesh part. Felt the deep-down pain. He could also feel blood drenching his back. The pain made him scream. His hands lost their grip on the steering wheel and the Land Rover wobbled. It veered to the side of the road, the front wheels bouncing over the edge of the grass verge. The heavy vehicle ran partway down the slope, then rolled onto its side. Len was thrown violently across the cab, the scorpion falling on top of him. He screamed even louder as it clung to him like some obscene leech. The jolt of the overturned Land Rover had inflamed the creature and it drew itself close to Len's squirming body, tearing at him in a frenzy. Blood began to spatter the inside of the cab. The scorpion's mutilation of Len's body continued long after he had ceased struggling.

* * *

Miles was speaking to Richard Groves via the radio in Braddock's car.

'. . . and we've admitted three more in

the last hour,' Groves was saying. 'Two police officers and a fireman. They were dealing with a couple of dead scorpions but hadn't taken all the precautions we've laid down.'

'Any luck with the vaccine?'

Groves's disappointment was echoed in his tone. 'No. Miles, we're struggling. I'm seriously thinking of calling for outside help. We need a department that has better facilities.'

'Whatever you think's best.'

'I'm trying to cover all angles,' Groves said. 'The problem is there isn't a pattern to any of this. Everything's too random. Too isolated. We have people being brought in suffering from stings. Or bites. And then those who've contracted the infection.'

'It's pretty well the same out here. This fire has sent the scorpions off in all directions. I think if they'd stayed on the moor the majority of them would have simply died from the infection. Now they're on the move, carrying the infection wherever they go. When the pain gets too much for them they seem to go berserk. They become totally aggressive. They're attacking now without logical cause. It isn't a defensive thing, or even for food. They simply need to strike out and kill.'

'I don't envy you being out there, Miles.'

'Keeps me off the streets,' Miles grinned. 'I'll be in touch.'

As Miles finished speaking a uniformed constable approached the car. Braddock rolled down his window.

'Message for you from HQ in Penzance, sir. In the communications van,' the constable said, indicating the dark-blue police vehicle parked at the side of the road.

Braddock nodded. 'I'm on my way. As he climbed out of the car he said: 'Ranleigh, would you tune back to the helicopter and listen for any calls?'

Miles watched Braddock make his way across to the mobile communications centre. Beyond where the vehicles were parked, across the open moorland, he could see the rolling clouds of smoke and the glimmer of flames rising above the undulating landscape.

The radio hummed softly, crackling every once in a while. Miles looked up when he heard a precise click. Seconds later the familiar voice of the helicopter pilot issued from the speaker.

'Sky-One to Control. Sky-One to Control. Over.'

Miles picked up the mike. 'Control to Sky-One. I hear you.'

'That you, Mr Ranleigh?'

'Yes.'

'I've sighted a group of scorpions. Must be seven or eight of them.'

'Where?'

'They're at a cottage a few miles from where you are. One on its own. Stands back off the road. Has a gravel drive. Just off the . . .'

'Sky-One, I know the place,' Miles shouted. 'Can you land nearby?'

'No. Too many trees in the area. Closest I can touch down is at least a mile away.'

'*Try*!' Miles yelled. 'There's someone in that cottage!'

He dropped the mike and kicked open

the door. On his feet he ran for the Range Rover. There was no time to tell Braddock. He would just have to pick up the message when he left the communications van.

All Miles could think about was Jill, alone in the cottage surrounded by a group of scorpions. He called himself every kind of a fool for not insisting that she leave the area. But until the fire had started driving the scorpions towards town she hadn't been in any immediate danger. Things had happened so quickly since the fire that he hadn't had time to consider the fact that Jill might suddenly be in the scorpions' path. He dreaded the thought of what might confront him when he arrived at the cottage.

The Range Rover hit the tarmac road, the rear end slithering before Miles brought the heavy vehicle under control. Then he slammed his foot hard down and sent the big motor howling along the road.

Driving one-handed he grabbed a box of shotgun cartridges and fumbled it open. He stuffed every available pocket with the things. The shotgun on the seat beside him was fully loaded, so he was as ready as he could be.

The road seemed endless. He was going so fast he missed the turning that led him onto the road prior to the cottage. Miles stamped on the brake and the Range Rover slithered to a stop in a cloud of dust. Reversing he moved past the opening, knocked the gears into first and took the corner with a squeal of protesting rubber.

He was doing close on sixty as he approached the cottage. The double gates were closed. Miles didn't hesitate. He yanked the Rover's wheel round and the powerful vehicle smashed through the gates in a shower of splintered wood. The skidding Rover rammed one of the gateposts in passing, tearing a long gash down the side of the body. The gravel drive lay in front of Miles, the big Jaguar parked up near the cottage.

He saw the scorpions. Five of them clustered near the front door. The door was open, the wood torn and splintered. *The pilot said seven or eight*. Miles swung the Rover and aimed it at the grouped scorpions. He felt the solid thump of contact. Jamming on the brakes he brought the vehicle to a slithering halt, throwing open the door before it had stopped moving. Snatching up the shotgun he rolled out of the seat.

A scorpion appeared and in the instant before he pulled the trigger Miles saw that the creature was in a terrible condition. Its body was overrun with dripping sores. Dark fluid dribbled from its open mouth. Yet even in such an advanced state of the infection there was no mistaking the menacing attitude. It scuttled forward.

The shotgun bellowed loudly, the blast ripping open the festering body. The scorpion's head disintegrated, leaving behind a shredded mess that oozed grey-green.

As the scorpion flopped to the ground Miles circled away. He couldn't be sure how many he'd killed with the vehicle. The question was answered seconds later when two scorpion heads showed at the rear of the Rover.

Miles didn't hesitate. He triggered a shot at one and saw it burst apart. The other drew back.

Miles ran to the front of the Range Rover. He scrambled up onto the bonnet, moving to the far side. He was able to look down on the scorpion lurking near the rear of the vehicle. Miles leaned out a little and fired. The creature arched almost double as the charge of shot ripped into its body. It twisted over onto its back, legs twitching violently.

Jumping down Miles took a look under the Rover. Two crushed scorpions lay beneath the vehicle's large wheels. *At least that accounted for the ones outside*.

He ran for the front door. From somewhere in the cottage he heard a scream. It seemed to go on and on, the sound making his blood run cold.

Miles scanned the area just inside the door, the shotgun up and ready. He was sweating profusely.

A faint sound reached his ears. Coming from the left. Miles recalled that part of the cottage, an open cloakroom, had polished wood flooring. The sound repeated itself. A brittle scratching . . .

Miles spun on his heel. The lurking scorpion lunged forward, feet scrabbling for a grip on the wood-block floor. Miles fired a hasty shot. The charge ripped off one of the scorpion's flexing claws. The creature came on. Desperately Miles reloaded, aimed . . . the scorpion almost collided with him . . . the shotgun's charge gouged a long furrow in the floor. Splinters of wood filled the air. Miles breathed in the foul stench of the rotting body as it slithered by him. He twisted, praying that he would be able to bring the shotgun round in time to . . . he saw, out of the corner of his eye, the venom-dripping sting at the tip of the swaying tail. A shudder coursed through his body. Miles threw himself backwards, ignoring the pain that flared as he hit the floor. He wrenched himself over, lying prone on his stomach, the shotgun thrust out before him. Miles fired. Saw the scorpion slide across the floor as the charge caught its side. He rose on one knee, fired and fired again, not content until the scorpion had been reduced to pulp . . .

He ran through the lounge. Furniture had been disturbed. A chair knocked over. A glass ornament lay smashed on the floor.

He heard noise above his head.

More screaming.

Upstairs.

He went up two at a time. Eyes searching. On the landing he stumbled. Went to his knees. Pushed against the wall to steady himself. Heard the low hiss of menace. His head rose, turned.

A huge scorpion — the thing must have been at least five and a half feet in length, looking even bigger as it rose on fully extended legs — came across the landing at him. Miles didn't have time to fire. He lashed out with the shotgun, striking at the head. The hard steel barrel connected with a solid impact. The scorpion drew back, only momentarily. Even as it did one claw snapped out, gripping Miles' left arm above the elbow. He felt the flesh tear. Blood streamed down his arm. Realising he only had a few seconds in which to act, he jerked the shotgun down firing an instant before the dripping sting began its strike. The scorpion's body exploded like a rotting melon. The force of the charge shoving it across the landing and through the railings edging the stairs.

Miles stumbled upright. His left arm hung uselessly at his side, blood dribbling from his fingers.

He heard a splintering crash coming from the front of the cottage.

Jill's bedroom!

He ran headlong down the long passage, emerged on the square, second landing, and saw the shattered door swinging loosely on its hinges . . .

He staggered to the door, leaning against the frame. In one swift glance he took in the scene.

Jill cowering in a corner of the room, pressed against the wall, her mouth open in a continuous scream of pure terror.

A lone, large scorpion moving towards her, poised and ready to strike.

Miles levelled the shotgun and pulled the trigger, blasting away the creature's legs. The scorpion writhed furiously. Lashing out with sting and claws, mouth snapping viciously, spilling its body fluids across the floor. Miles reloaded and fired again, tearing the thing's head clean off its body. Then again and again and again. Firing until the shotgun was empty and he was drained of all emotion.

The room stank of gunsmoke and decay.

Miles crossed the room and reached for Jill. She stopped screaming the moment he touched her, and her body trembled violently.

'Come on, let's get out of here,' he said gently.

He led her from the cottage, out into the warm sunlight of the late afternoon. As they walked slowly down toward the gate a line of police cars roared along the narrow road and skidded to a halt. Sam Braddock was one of the first to reach him.

'You all right?'

Miles nodded. 'We are now,' he said.

Jill turned her head to look at him. For the first time since he'd met her Miles saw her less than composed. Her pale face was streaked with tears. Her hair ruffled. Even so she still looked beautiful to him.

'Miles, your lovely Range Rover,' she said.

He glanced over his shoulder. 'Cars can be put back together,' he said. 'It isn't so easy to do that with people.'

Braddock came across to lean through the car window.

'I'd've given anything to have seen you do your John Wayne act,' he said.

'Don't expect another performance like that,' Miles answered. 'I daren't even think about it.'

'You saw the size of those two in the house?'

'I didn't have much time to run a tape-measure over them, but they were quite large.'

'*Quite large!* Jesus, I almost wet myself looking at them!'

Miles opened the car door. 'Inspector, I'm taking Jill through to Penzance. I want to get her away from here.'

'Go ahead,' Braddock said. 'I'll see to it that the cottage is cleaned up. You want someone to drive you?'

'No. I'm fine now.'

'I'll get someone to look at that arm

first,' Braddock said.

'I'd forgotten about it,' Miles said. He suddenly became aware of the pain that was pulsing fiercely. 'I think maybe you better had.'

'That call I had just before you left,' Braddock said. 'it was from the fire control. It appears they've managed to get on top of the fire. Looks like they'll stop it well short of town. Then it can just burn itself out.'

'All we have to worry about now are surviving scorpions.'

'Well we've had the moor area pretty well ringed since the fire. There have been a few incidents. On the other hand we've killed a fair number of scorpions. Add the ones you've killed here. It's only a feeling, Ranleigh, but I think we've about seen the last of them.'

'That's what we thought after Long Point.'

'I'm not being complacent. I won't be satisfied until we've checked and treble-checked. As soon as the fire's died down I'm going to have the moor combed thoroughly. See if we can total up how many died in the blaze.'

'Inspector, if you need me give me a call. I'll let you know where we're staying in Penzance.'

Braddock smiled. 'That information will keep for a couple of days at least.'

For the first time since Miles had brought her from the cottage Jill managed a pale smile. 'A minimum of a couple of days,' she said. '*At least that!*'

20

The only scorpions sighted in the following weeks were those which had died from the infection. Yet this still enabled the scorpions to kill. Despite the precautions laid down by the medical authorities there were always those who disregarded such advice. Those who failed to pay attention paid with their lives. It took over seven months before a vaccine was perfected. By then there was little need of it. Victims of the infection were dead and buried.

High Moor, after the fire, became a blackened wilderness. Teams of men, protected by heavy suits, tramped back and forth across the ravaged tract of land, searching for any signs that might indicate surviving scorpions. All they found were shrivelled corpses. The burned scorpions were dissected and the tissue closely studied. No sign of the baccillus was found. Ironically the fire, seemingly a threat to man at the outset, had done a great service. It had destroyed both the scorpions and the infection they carried.

Sam Braddock was true to his word. He maintained close checks on High Moor and the surrounding countryside for a full year. There were many false alarms. Calls from hoaxers which sent teams of police out to check for signs. Braddock refused to be put off. Everything was checked. Nothing was ever found. Even so Braddock kept an open mind on the subject. He never let himself forget that the Port Pendall incident had been started by a few of the original scorpions somehow transported from Kent to Cornwall. Everyone had believed the scorpion menace to be over after Long Point. They had been wrong then. Braddock had no wish for a similar mistake to occur because of his laxity.

One of Braddock's links in his safety-chain was Miles Ranleigh. The two men had become close friends, as well as co-workers in the aftermath of the outbreak. If Miles had to make any trips he always left word as to his whereabouts so Braddock could get in touch.

That was until the time Braddock put in a call to Miles, almost a year to the day of the High Moor fire. It was Jill who answered the phone.

'Hi, Sam.'

'Where's the great man?'

'He isn't here.'

Braddock detected the worry in her voice. 'So where is he?'

'Sam, I don't know.'

'But you always know.'

'Not this time. He got a phone call yesterday. Afterwards he became agitated. It isn't like Miles. He was all worked up over something. But he wouldn't tell me what. He simply threw some things into a bag and left.'

'And you don't know where?'

'Well not exactly. What I mean is I don't know the precise place.'

'But?'

'He made a call just before he left. They called back after he'd gone to confirm that he could make his connection after all when he reached Los Angeles International Airport. That's all I know, Sam. He's gone to the United States . . . '

THE END

Other titles in the
Linford Mystery Library:

THE TOUCH OF HELL

Michael R. Linaker

The village of Shepthorne wasn't being gripped, but strangled by winter's blanket of snow and Arctic temperatures. The trouble began with a massive pile-up on frozen roads and a fireball of exploding petrol as a truck collided with a tanker in the garage forecourt. Then, from the sky, a huge military transport with its cargo of devastation crashed down towards the village. Hell was just beginning to touch Shepthorne . . .

SWEET SISTER DEATH

Frederick Nolan

The objective of PACT — a secret counter-terrorism organisation, is to eradicate the perpetrators of political assassination and terrorist acts, and Charles Garrett is their best weapon. A bizarre series of murders plunges Garrett into a deadly conspiracy mounted by the terrorist Leila Jarhoun — the leader of a suicide cell created to unleash a holocaust of death across Europe. Jarhoun always strikes where Garrett least expects, until finally she confronts him — three hundred and fifty feet above New York harbour . . .

THY ARM ALONE

John Russell Fearn

Betty Shapley was a local beauty, for whose charms three young men fell heavily. But her coquetry would lead to death for one of her admirers, Herbert Pollitt; a fugitive's life for another, Vincent Grey; and becoming a murder-case witness for the third, Tom Clayton. Inspector Morgan and Sergeant Claythorne investigate the death, and suspect Vincent Grey. So Betty, former pupil of Roseway College for Young Ladies, asks Miss Maria Black — 'Black Maria', the headmistress detective — to prove Grey's innocence.

MAN IN DUPLICATE

John Russell Fearn

Playboy millionaire Harvey Bradman is set an ultimatum by his fiancée: before she marries him, he must carry out some significant, courageous act. Amazingly, the next day the newspaper carries a full report of Harvey's heroic rescue of a woman from her stalled car on a level crossing, avoiding a rail crash! But Harvey had been asleep in bed at the time of the incident. And when his mysterious twin seeks him out, he becomes enmeshed in a sinister conspiracy . . .